Fairy Tale Princesses Will Kill Your Children

Jane Gilmore

www.JaneGilmore.com

We acknowledge that Aboriginal and Torres Strait Islander peoples are the Traditional Custodians and the first storytellers of the lands on which we live and work. We honour Aboriginal and Torres Strait Islander peoples' continuous connection to Country, waters, skies and communities. We celebrate Aboriginal and Torres Strait Islander stories, traditions and living cultures; and we pay our respects to Elders past and present.

First published by Jane Gilmore, 2023

Cover artwork by Janine Marshall

Cover design by Phoenix Waddell

A catalogue record for this book is available from the National Library of Australia

*For Witch Carson,
in thanks for reminding me that
there is always more to learn.*

With heartfelt thanks to Kate Leaver, Keira O'Reilly, Janine Marshall, Phoenix Waddell, Barbara Gilmore, and Deanne Carson. I wouldn't have been able to do this without you.

About the Author

Jane Gilmore is an award winning journalist, turned author and consent educator. She has been researching and writing about the causes and effects of violence and poverty for over a decade and is now also delivering consent and respectful relationships education in Australian schools.

Her first book, *Fixed It: Violence and the Representation of Women in the Media* was published in 2019. Her second book, *Teaching Consent: Real Voices from the Consent Classroom* was published in 2022.

You can purchase all her books direct from her website or order from your local book store.

www.JaneGilmore.com/books

Contents

"What so many of us learn far too late is that there's a huge difference between the stories girls are told to aspire to, and the ones boys are taught they deserve. For us, the boy is the quest. For them, the girl is just the reward."

Clementine Ford, I Don't: The Case Against Marriage, 2023

Princess Myths in the Modern World

I've been writing about men's violence and women's poverty for more than 15 years. I've sat in courtrooms and newsrooms and kitchens and refuges, listening to women recount horrors and talk about shame. I've sat in those same courtrooms, newsrooms, and kitchens and listened as the men who enacted horrors talk about their rights. However furious, frustrated, or exhausted I've been, I've never stopped wanting to understand what creates women's shame and feeds men's entitlement.

In eight years of the *Fixed It* project, I've been documenting the media's comprehensive refusal to recognise that men are responsible for their choice to rape, kill, and abuse women and children. Thousands of articles, hundreds of public events, dozens of media appearances, three books, one master's degree later, and I have seen some encouraging improvements in laws, attitudes, and beliefs about gender. But I can also see how much more we need to do to disrupt the myths that fuel men who harm women and the structures that enable them.

What does this have to do with Snow White? A lot more than I thought before I started this book.

A couple of years ago, I watched Disney's 1937 animation of the Snow White story. I can't remember why I decided to watch it, but I clearly remember how horrified I was that blatant misogyny could be displayed so casually in a movie made for children. Digging into the origins of the story left me even more horrified. The Grimm Brother's fairy tale about seven-year-old Snow White and her tragic stepmother kept me awake at night. A woman so driven by fear and jealousy that she would kill a child, and a man so devoid of humanity that he would fall in love with that dead child. These were the villains and heroes fed to generations of little girls to shape their expectations of the world and themselves. I rewrote the Grimm Brother's *Little Snow White* story one cold, wet night when all I had for company was boredom and a bottle of red wine. I didn't try to change her fate, or that of her far more interesting stepmother. I simply reworded it to highlight the fear and hatred of women that was soaked into every word. It was immensely satisfying, one of the rare times that writing felt like a gift rather than a form of self-harm, so I kept going.

After *Snow White*, Disney released *Cinderella* in 1950, *Sleeping Beauty* in 1959, *The Little Mermaid* in 1989, and *Beauty and the Beast* in 1991. These were, for many years, what Disney called their "top five princesses". While each princess was given specific colours, styles and (most importantly) marketing campaigns, they all embody the same myth: if girls are beautiful, unselfish, and always afraid of older women, a Handsome Prince will bestow his love upon her, and she will live happily ever after. While it's tempting to dismiss this trope as a thing of the past, streaming services provide today's children with effortless access to these fairy tales, and who would think their children are in danger if they're sitting down in front of the Disney channel?

On current growth, the Disney Plus streaming channel will have a subscriber base of over 200 million people by the end of 2023 and the company anticipates increasing that to 300 million by the end of 2025. Almost half the accounts are kids under seven years of age, and their users are split evenly between male and female (they do not record any other genders).

So, using this as a guide, I took Disney's "top five princesses" as a basis and wrote my way through all of them.

Other than identifying older women as the only threat to young girls, each story is about the Princess's path to true happiness in the form of marriage to the Handsome Prince. His love, earned by youthful beauty and submissive sweetness, rescues the Princess from poverty, oppression, and the torture of being unwed. Evil is personified in older women driven by bitter jealousy of beautiful young girls and the princess overcomes evil, not by fighting it, but by proving how sweet and kind they can be in the face of it.

Apart from her beauty, the fairy tale princess's defining quality is her unselfishness – meaning she does not want anything or ask for anything or object to anything. She exists only to create happiness for others and the more she can erase her own feelings and desires, the more worthy she is of the ultimate reward - the Handsome Prince. Unselfishness in fairy tales is the greatest of feminine virtues, possibly even more important than beauty. Failing to achieve unselfishness is often punished with violence and always results in being rejected by Handsome Princes and suffering that worst of fates, remaining unwed.

The Handsome Prince will only come for the most perfectly beautiful, pure, submissive girl in the world. She must suffer uncomplaining at the hands of her enemies (other women) and remain in perfect isolation, befriended only by birds and fluffy animals. She can only deserve wealth and power if she doesn't want it or work for it. And only The Handsome Prince can bestow wealth and happiness upon her as a reward for her natural beauty and unselfishness.

Beauty and the Beast was the first Disney film to introduce a villainous male character in Gaston, the smugly threatening handsome man who is adored by all the villagers. He even gets his own ditty, where all the denizens of the tavern join him in song to extol his virtues as a man, an icon, and a role model. It is a bit tongue in cheek, slightly ridiculing the villagers for their hero-worship, but they are never called upon to reject him or hold him accountable for his failings. The true evil - the curse on the Handsome Prince - comes from a sorceress disguised as an ugly old woman. The Handsome Prince is saved by Beauty's loving unselfishness, but Gaston brings about his own demise through hubris and cowardice. This looks like just deserts but in fact, it's the opposite. Gaston's self-inflicted demise is reassurance for all the smugly threatening men of the time, handsome or not, who almost never suffered any consequences for their hubris and cowardice and could therefore continue to believe in the myth of their own heroism.

It's not fair or accurate to say that Disney princesses are all as helpless and passive as the first five. Many of the later princesses aspired to be more than just a good, submissive woman but until very recently, their stories were still about their path to the Handsome Prince and the happy ever after only he could give them.

In the early 2000s, Disney left the passive princess trope behind and turned to the princess version of the Manic Pixie Dream Girl. She is bookish, quirky, and adorably clumsy. Her greatest feature is that she is "not like other girls" and her purpose is to be a tool that turns slightly dodgy men into heroes. The Manic Pixie Dream Princess often shows a veneer of independence but typically ends up in peril and is rescued by the Handsome Prince as he reaches the end of his hero's journey.

Tangled's Rapunzel was clumsy, naive, talkative, and whimsical – the perfect Manic Pixie Dream Princess. Her villain was a cruel and controlling old woman, so driven by her fear of aging that she kidnapped and imprisoned a child. Rapunzel escaped with the help of her slightly dodgy man and then tumbled around the kingdom, charming violent men (who were really just loveable rogues) and being so adorable that the slightly dodgy man is transformed into a Handsome Prince, and they live happily ever after.

In 2013, *Frozen*, acclaimed at the time as Disney finally achieving feminist cred, created another Manic Pixie Dream Princess in Anna. She is charming and clumsy, given to inconsequential chatter and intuitive leaps. She saves her sister and wins her "fixer upper" Handsome Prince. Elsa's story is much more interesting. While the Handsome Prince is the villain, Elsa's true antagonist is herself and her fear of her own power. She is not saved by a man; she's saved by her sister's love and she wins her happy ever after by embracing the power she was born to and the power she creates. Even so, Elsa and Anna are both conventionally beautiful princesses who learn that unselfish service to others is their great achievement.

Today, few (if any) parents would give the original Grimm Brothers fairy tales to their children. The Disney versions of these stories, however, are still easily accessible. Disney is a profit-making enterprise, not an instrument of social change. They commodify storytelling by reflecting the world, not changing it. Their stories have become more complex since the 1930s because modern children have much more sophisticated expectations of the stories they consume, but Disney is following the change, not leading it. In the last year or two, they've shown the capacity to do this remarkably well. *Encanto* is an adorable delight of a film, featuring wonderfully drawn women and girls who have complex inner lives and ambitions. They spend time with loving and protective older women who have flaws, traumatic pasts, difficult emotions, and brown skin. They all have a future to look forward to and these futures are not limited to seeking happiness through marriage. Despite this very recent change, Disney's extensive back catalogue is still available on their streaming service, masquerading as harmless entertainment for millions of children to watch and absorb.

All of Disney's "top five" princesses were white. Their next few Princesses explored stories of women of colour, but even when Princesses were allowed to be something other than white, they still had to be beautiful, innocent, self-sacrificing, and always find the peak of their ambitions at the altar with their Handsome Prince. Jasmine from *Aladdin* (1992), *Pocahontas* (1995), *Mulan* (1998), and Tiana from *The Princess and the Frog* (2009) are all as problematic as you would expect from films made by white dudes trying to prove their white saviour cred by retrofitting fairy tales to tell women of colour's stories. While those stories also are not mine to tell, it's impossible to talk about patriarchy without talking about race.

I think of patriarchy as a pyramid. Power is centred at the top, defined by sexuality, race, class, physicality, and gender. The apex of power is the straight, white, wealthy, able-bodied man. Every deviation from his identity pushes you further down the pyramid. Your power in the world is dependent on making sure the people below you cannot move up while you fight the people above you for space. The pyramid is multifaceted because power is never dependent on one single facet of your identity, all of them work together to determine your access to power.

Straight, white, wealthy, able-bodied men don't have to fight anyone above them, but they do have to protect their position from the people (i.e. everyone else) below them. They do it with violence and economics, and politics. With misinformation and gender roles and racial stereotypes. Job descriptions and pay scales and insecure work. News reports and rules of evidence and prison sentences. Private schools and marriage rituals and menstrual shame. Fashion trends and pockets in your clothes and comfortable shoes. Medical research and healthcare access and inaccessible buildings. Disney films and princess myths and impossible beauty standards.

The Grimm Brothers played a very deliberate part in maintaining this pyramid. They were German nationalists who advocated for the unification of the German states and believed that collecting old German folktales would aid in promoting a national culture. Their stories were rife with violence and anti-Semitism (several stories featured avaricious and treacherous characters called "The Jew" who were punished in a variety of ways). The Nazis later used the Grimm Brothers stories as propaganda, interpreting Cinderella's Aryan beauty as a sign of her racial purity, while the evil stepsisters symbolised the supposed Jewish threat. In most imaginings of Cinderella since the Grimm Brothers, she looks like an enchanted-era Taylor Swift. (And before a thousand enraged Swifties take to their keyboards, I am a proud Swiftie myself. Mostly for her music and storytelling genius, but also because I love how she wrapped herself in the princess daydream and subverted it into the patriarchy's worst nightmare: an intelligent, ambitious woman who rejects marriage and has the power to choose the success of her own creativity as her happy ever after.)

All traditional fairy tales are very clear on the gender binary - at the time there was no recognition in Western culture that gender could be conceived any other way. Girls were girls, boys were boys, and violent punishment is immediate and righteous for anyone who steps outside their assigned gender ideal. In recent decades, many writers and artists from the LQBTIQA+ community have played with these ideas, giving different genders and sexualities to various fairy tale characters, or disrupting the assumptions about straight cis princes and princesses. It's a fascinating and creative genre, but in my retellings (where I created a new story for my princesses) I wanted them to have ambitions beyond romance. The whole point of it seemed to me to be giving them choices and opportunities to discover and explore all aspects of themselves and then leave their future undecided. If I wrote their path, then whatever I chose for them would be their only option. If I could wish anything for them, or for anyone, it would be limitless options.

It struck me when I was reading the Grimm version of Cinderella that she is one of the few princesses who has a name. Grimm Brothers' princesses were more likely to have descriptions such as 'king's daughter' or 'beautiful maiden'. Cinderella, however, was not actually her name, it was a scornful epithet given to her by her stepsisters because she was made to sleep in the ashes of the kitchen fire and "on that account she always looked dirty and dusty". One of the many trends I've noticed in doing the *Fixed It* project for so long is how often women are defined by what they do ('influencer', 'sex worker') or their relationship to a man ('wife of', 'daughter of'). As long as they're not accused of violence, men always have names. For example, 'Hugh Jackman announced split from wife' was a headline over a recent article about Deborra Lee Furness and Hugh Jackman's joint announcement of the end of their marriage.

While I couldn't re-write Cinderella as a woman of colour, I could reject her Aryan heritage and her nameless past, so I called her Anvika, which the internet tells me is a Hindu name meaning powerful and complete. My Anvika is not intended to be of any specific race, her name simply invites readers to consider that the heroine does not have to be white. And yes, it did give me a bit of joy that Nazis would hate the very suggestion that their Aryan princess could have a Hindu name because who doesn't find joy in upsetting Nazis?

Disney and the Grimm Brothers may have imagined their Sleeping Beauty as a beautiful blonde, but in her origin story she was far more likely to be a brown-eyed brunette. In 1634, Italian poet Giambattista Basile published *Sun, Moon and Talia*, an adaptation of *Perceforest*, a French romance first printed in 1528. In Basile's version the princess is poisoned by an old woman, her father thinks she is dead, leaves her body in a house and flees. The hero is a Handsome King who finds and explores the house. What happened next is best told in a translation of the Basile original:

> "At last he came to the saloon, and when the king beheld Talia, who seemed as one ensorcelled,

he believed that she slept, and he called her, but she remained insensible, and crying aloud, he felt his blood course hotly through his veins in contemplation of so many charms; and he lifted her in his arms, and carried her to a bed, whereon he gathered the first fruits of love, and leaving her upon the bed, returned to his own kingdom, where, in the pressing business of his realm, he for a time, thought no more of this incident."

Sun, Moon and Talia, Giambattista Basile, 1634

Nine months after the king raped Talia and then got too busy to remember it, she gave birth to twins, one of whom sucked on her finger and removed the poison. Talia woke up and was delighted to find that she had given birth, despite having no memory of their father. Not long after that, the King remembered the woman he raped and returned to the house, presumably to rape her again. Talia was delighted to meet the rapey King and they had a fun-filled few days together before he went back to his kingdom and his wife – yes he was married – who then became the villain of the story. The Queen ordered her servants to kill the babies, cook them, and feed them to the King. Then she tried to burn Talia alive, but the King arrived in time to rescue Talia from the flames. Loyal servants had hidden the babies instead of cooking them, so the King threw his wife into the fire, which meant he was free to marry Talia, and they all lived happily ever after.

What a fun story.

I struggled with *Sleeping Beauty*. I couldn't bring myself to write a rape story. And I couldn't leave my Talia to sleep through her own fairy tale, passively waiting for life to happen to her. I had to write a new story for her, one that gave her a much bigger and better future than a Handsome Prince. Creating a princess who doesn't need saving, doesn't have to glorify unselfishness, and who can look forward to a future full of possibilities was more than satisfying. It felt redemptive.

The Little Mermaid was published by Hans Christian Anderson in 1837. Again, she had a description but no name. She loved to talk and sing, she wanted to find love and she wanted a life more varied than the one she'd seen as a child. So, she was tortured and mutilated by an evil old witch as a lesson to little girls on the evils of talking and wanting. I spent so much time thinking about her that I couldn't rewrite her as a passive victim, so I rewrote her story as a coming-of-age moment, complete with wise and loving older women who did not prevent her bad choices but were there to help her recover and rebuild herself. Another immensely satisfying project.

Coercive control is a relatively new term for a tale as old as time, and it finds its embodiment in *Beauty and the Beast*. The story, first published in 17th century France, is a direct descendent of the Ancient Greek myth, *Cupid and Psyche*, first written down by Apuleius, an African born novelist in 2nd century Rome. It almost certainly has origins in oral storytelling traditions that go much further back, and variations of the story have appeared in most cultures around the world, such as *The Woman Who Married a Snake* in Indian folklore, the Chinese *Fairy Serpent*, and Russia's *The Scarlet Flower*. They all tell the tale of a father who is threatened, bribed, or blackmailed into giving his youngest daughter to a rich and brutal man as restitution for theft. Most variations of the story include older sisters who are selfish, bold, or avaricious, and are therefore unworthy of the love of a Handsome Prince. The youngest daughter is submissive and hard-working, and unhesitatingly agrees to marriage with the Beast to save her father from the consequences of his theft. The Beast is actually a Handsome Prince, cursed by an evil witch or sorceress to appear violent and terrifying. Only a fairy tale Princess who remains steadfastly unselfish and loving in the face of his violence can free him from the geas that binds him to violence. His violence is written as her failure to love him enough and anyone who has ever had the misfortune to be "loved" by a violent man will tell you this story is not at all a thing of the past.

The villains in fairy tales are women who have power or agency. They are the wicked witches, evil queens, cruel stepmothers, and jealous stepsisters that bedevil all fairy tale princesses. Any woman who has gained some power in the world must be either malevolent and cruel or an evil temptress, luring a good man from his true path. They can be beautiful, but only if their evil natures are demonstrated by being sexually desirable rather than the pure, sexless beauty of the princess. If they're not seductive, they must be old, symbolising the morally culpable failure of femininity displayed by women who get older but refuse to become invisible.

Fairy tales have been around, in various forms, for as long as humans have had language. Stories are how we learn about the world and our place in it. They teach us empathy, values, consequences, critical thinking, and give us insight into lives unlike our own. Ancient cultures had long traditions of oral storytelling and they were absorbed and adapted by new groups, passed on by travellers and conquerors, passed back as conquered people were assimilated into new empires. Ancient Britons, Greeks, Africans, Indians, Samoan, and Mayan cultures breathed in the stories of those who came before them and breathed them out on the cultures that came after. We will never know what stories Neanderthal mothers told their children at night, but we can be sure that traces of those stores are still embedded in our cultural DNA.

Modern stories are more sophisticated than fireside tales of the past. CGIed, subtitled, streamed into our devices and consumed in planes, trains and automobiles, but they still serve the same purpose. Stories help us find answers to unanswerable questions: Who am I? What do I need to know about the world? What is happiness? What is death? How do I find one and avoid the other?

Stories are also how adults try to teach children about these questions and how to answer them. We use them to entertain and distract while we impart what we hope is wisdom and the values we think will keep them safe and happy. Fear or love of gods, countries, rulers, the possessions they can aspire to, the relationships that will protect and sustain them, the qualities they should have to achieve these ends. The wide-reaching storytellers of the last few centuries, the Grimm Brothers, Hans Christian Andersen, and the Disney Corporation among them, achieved success partly because the parents who buy stories believe their underlying values will be good for their children. Catering to those parents is why the Grimm Brothers stripped all the sex and some of the violence out of their stories. In the following century, Disney sanitised the stories even further, toning down the violence and adding songs, fairy godmothers, and dancing cutlery to their animated retelling of the Princess stories. The original stories, however, are still sitting at the dark centre of modern myths.

All the "top five" princesses have distant and uninterested fathers. Fairy tale kings make no effort to help their daughters as they are beset by evil, but this is never presented as a failing of fatherhood or masculinity. Even when they trade their daughters to terrifying Beasts, they are simply playing out "natural" fatherly acts. The fairy tale king is oblivious to his daughter's danger and merely waits for her to be rescued by marriage to the Handsome Prince. He never suffers any of the punishments reserved for the evil women of fairy tales. His role is to progenerate a daughter and bestow the title of princess upon her. He is not a morality tale for men and boys, or a warning to women and girls because fatherhood's only moral obligation is to provide wealth. Any failing of care, protection or guidance belongs to women.

The Handsome Prince is the apotheosis of every fairy tale princess's story, but he, too, is an archetype not a person. He might participate in a physical fight to demonstrate his masculine ability to rescue his princess from danger, but the villains he fights are not his protagonists, they're hers. He has no need of villains to overcome because he has no character development. He's a cipher, he exists only to be the key to female happiness and saves pure young princesses from the perils of unmarried life. He is never expected to learn the benefits of unselfishness, because men are allowed, even encouraged to have ambitions for themselves and their futures. Princesses are punished for such things. If the Handsome Prince is violent, angry, feckless, or boorish, he doesn't have to learn or improve himself, he simply waits for his princess to change him and then gives her the happy ever after her unselfishness has earned.

Demonising powerful women, who through age, experience, personality, or sheer force of their own desires have found agency outside winning a man's love, serves the needs of patriarchal power structures by strengthening the myth that "good" women are passive and isolated, completely dependent on their husbands. "Bad" women are active, independent, closely connected to other women like themselves, and in fairy tales, will always be served their just punishment of violence and death.

The mothers of all five princesses die before the story begins to ensure the princess myth is reinforced by the erasure of any loving protective womanhood. Dead, loving mothers are replaced by an evil mother figure who is the pivotal point of the fairy tale. The Princess must reject (but not fight) the evilness of "selfish" women to achieve her happily ever after, which can only happen when she is married to the Handsome Prince.

Even without the prince, what kind of goal is living happily ever after? Life without grief, effort, work, even moments of boredom or self-doubt, in some untouched Stepford world of ease and nothingness is not just unrealistic, it's deeply unsatisfying. A woman who is fully engaged with herself, her children (if she chooses to have them), and the wider world will always have moments of pain and exhilaration and quiet achievement. Women with ambition and desires would want, even need such experiences.

But this is an essential aspect of the fairy tale princess myth: she doesn't have a future. Her story ends at the altar. If it didn't, what would happen after she marries her Handsome Prince and has his children? Does she become the beautiful Queen who dies after giving birth to a daughter? Does her Handsome Prince become the King whose second wife is the villain in her daughter's story of helpless femininity? We are never told because motherhood is not patriarchy's aspirational fairy tale and fairy tale princess stories must end before the princess outgrows her teens. Older women are the villains, not the heroines, of fairy tales.

It would be so comforting to believe that these attitudes disappeared with all the social and legislative changes women fought to achieve over the last 50 years. Reality, however, is rarely comforting. There are hundreds of research papers from all over the world that prove rape myths are still the most effective form of defence in a rape trial. The most recent one I found is from August 2023. The New South Wales Bureau of Crime Statistics and Research conducted analysis of transcripts from 75 sexual offence trials and found rape myths were "regularly relied upon" in almost all trials.

Rape myths are the natural descendants of the princess myth. They say that rape is only 'real rape' when a beautiful, naïve, young woman is attacked by a stranger who is instantly recognisable as a monster. She screams, fights back, and receives visible physical injuries. She reports immediately to police and remembers every detail in its exact chronological order. She cries but is never angry and tears are the only signs of trauma she ever displays. The domestic violence myth is rape myth's evil stepsister, in which another young, beautiful, unworldly woman is manipulated into marriage by a recognisably monstrous man who isn't white, well-educated, or wealthy. She does not fight back, but she also reports to police, cries without anger, and shows no other signs of trauma. Any deviation from these scripts is proof that she is a liar out to ruin a man's life, probably as vengeance for his sexual rejection of her.

The wicked witch trope is another close relative of rape and domestic violence myths. Any woman who has power in the form of age, knowledge, expertise, or wisdom can be cast as a witch. While the dangerous old woman archetype existed before the Middle Ages and outside Europe, it became so personified by the Wicked Witch that up to 50,000 women were tortured, raped, and killed (often by being burnt alive) by men who were lauded for their work in protecting "good" women and girls from their evil influence. Fairy tales were common entertainment at the time, but the wicked witch blurred the lines of fiction and what at the time was claimed as fact.

Malleus Malefica (translates as Hammer of the Witches) was the main treatise on witchcraft during the witch hunt era (roughly 1450 to 1750). Written by a German Catholic clergyman, the Malefica recommends torture to obtain confessions, and execution as the only possible sentence after confession were acquired. It also explains why most witches were women:

> "They are more credulous ... more impressionable . .. they have slippery tongues ... she is more carnal than a man ... they are more prone to abjure the faith ... women also have weak memories . .. and it is a

normal vice in her not to be disciplined .... As she is a liar by nature, so in her speech she stings while she delights us… There was a defect in the formation of the first woman, since she was formed from a bent rib ... which is bent in the contrary direction to a man. And since through this defect she is an imperfect animal, she always deceives."
Henricus Institor, Malleus Malefica, 1486

Matthew Hale was one of English history's most famous judges. He was a devout Puritan who enthusiastically endorsed witch trials during the 1600s. He sentenced several women to death for witchcraft and wrote about presiding over these trials as great act of piety and service to god. Hale, like many pious misogynists, was also deeply concerned about women being 'malicious and false witnesses' against men of 'good character'. He described rape as 'an accusation easily to be made and hard to be proved, and harder to be defended by the party accused, tho never so innocent'. In 1973, this statement was described by a US appellate judge as 'one of the most oft-quoted passages in our jurisprudence'. Hale was also the source of the common law rule (later legislated) that a man could not rape his wife because, he said, 'by their mutual matrimonial consent and contract the wife has given herself up in this kind to her husband, which she cannot retract'. Wicked witches, pure princesses and evil sorceresses do not live only in fairy tales. They haunt our courtrooms and live large in the minds of our juries.

There's only a very small step from the courtroom to the news media. Most of the journalism about men's violence against women comes from court and crime reporting, which is restricted to reporting what was said in court with no commentary or context. If trials are run on rape and domestic violence myths, the reporting on those trials must follow the same line. Is there doubt that a woman is a fairy tale princess? Could she be an evil stepsister or a wicked witch? If so, she is guilty of cursing the Handsome Prince with a rape trial and she must be punished. The trial is to test her guilt, not his.

The princess myth doesn't end with the legal system. It is also interwoven into our economy, how we value and pay for work, who we value and pay for work.

Snow White works for the seven dwarves because she loves doing unpaid domestic labour. She whistles while she works and sings a jaunty little song about how cheerfully she can tidy up a house because cleaning is so much fun if you can dance with your broom and imagine it is your Handsome Prince.

Cinderella also understands her role in domestic labour but not being born a princess, her dream is about the boundaries of class. Her unselfish nature, a beautiful dress and a Handsome Prince save her from a life of drudgery and set the terms for all women – you can marry into wealth, but you cannot earn it.

Fairy tale princesses do not seek independence, they love domestic work and are too unselfish to demand acknowledgment or appreciation for their work.

Even though most women in countries like Australia either stop paid work or change to part time work after they marry and have children, "official" gender pay gaps are calculated by only looking at full time salaries, often deceptively described as what people "earn" rather than what they are paid. By the time women are in their thirties, they are three times more likely to be doing paid work either part time or not at all. When they reach their fifties, Australian Tax Office data shows they are, on average, paid less than half the annual amount paid to men of the same age. Those women, approaching the age of wicked witches and evil crones, are the fast-growing cohort of homeless people in the country and I very much doubt they "choose" low-paid or unpaid work over having somewhere safe to live.

I work in the domestic violence sector, which is the most female dominated workforce in Australia other than childcare. Both professions are the lowest paid of any skilled jobs, and as anyone working on the front-line of domestic violence services will tell you, it's dangerous work. The women doing that psychologically dangerous work are underpaid and undervalued because the premise of their expertise is rejecting fairy tale myths and acting on the reality of men's violence against women. The women caring for children are doing work prescribed by the fairy tale myth (caring for small children) and must therefore unselfishly accept poverty and housing insecurity as their allotted fate until they can earn their rescue by a Handsome Prince.

Whistle while you work ladies, because princesses will only be rescued by the Handsome Prince if they love dancing with their brooms and look beautiful in their simple gowns.

Unpaid, undervalued work. Class barriers. Consent. Control. Silence. Good (unselfish) girls. Evil (selfish) women. Fairy tale prince and princess myths are seeded into the DNA of our laws, politics, economics, and media. Rooting them out is not easy or quick, but we cannot even start if we don't recognise them and the harm they do to all of us.

I think that's why feminist retelling of fairy tales has such a long and wonderful history. It was fashionable in 17th century France and had a resurgence during the feminist revolution in the 1970s as second wave feminists rejected the blissfully happy housewife myth that fit so well into the fairy tale morality of marriage. The genre has never disappeared and there are examples of it scattered across various forms of storytelling in the last 50 years.

My contribution to the genre has a very specific purpose: exposing the myths embedded in fairy tales that I've seen play out so devastatingly in my work on men's violence and women's poverty. The key theme of Fixed It is that the most dangerous ideas are the ones we don't notice, particularly when they permeate our internal landscape. Once you recognise an idea and see it in all its glorious ridiculousness, it loses most of its power to hurt you or to cause you to hurt others. Fairy tale princesses are dangerous ideas. We need recognise them as treacherous myths that can hurt, even kill, our children, and give storytelling power to the women and girls who can defeat them: complex, ambitious, flawed, characters who strive for achievements in their own right, rather than fixing their success on someone else's happiness.

Little Snow White

In the original folktale about Snow White, which even the Grimm Brothers had to sanitise, Snow White's evil queen was not her stepmother but her mother. The queen had wished for a beautiful daughter but became so jealous of that daughter's beauty, she ordered a huntsman to take her child to the forest, cut out her lungs and liver, and bring them back for the queen to eat to restore her lost youth and beauty.

The Grimm Brothers edited out the cannibalistic mother, but their Little Snow White was only seven years old, and they had no qualms about marrying her off to the Handsome Prince. Their prose is very plain and didactic, which I have emulated, and some lines are quoted directly from the Grimm Brother's version, because not even I could make this stuff up. I've underlined the quotes I took from the original version for those of you who may have read it so long ago that you don't remember how truly awful it was.

I did not attempt to change the plot or Little Snow White's fate as dictated by the Grimm Brothers. I simply reworded their version to highlight the ideas they were trying to convey to their audience.

Once upon a time there lived a King and Queen who longed for a child to inherit the throne and all their wealth. Eventually the Queen gave birth to a baby girl. The King was too busy to be pleased about a daughter who wasn't a son but he named the baby Snow White so everyone would know she was white and pure and could therefore be beautiful. It's very important for girls to be beautiful but princesses do not exist if they are not beautiful. Luckily, Snow White was as beautiful as the day is long and days are very long for beautiful girls.

After Little Snow White was born the Queen died because women's stories always end when they have children.

Little Snow White was left to the care of her father, the King. Kings are far too busy doing important things with war and money to care for little girls, so he found a new Queen. "You are my wife," he said to her, "and you are beautiful. It is your task to raise my child and maintain your beauty, for your purpose is to show all the men in my kingdom that I am very powerful."

The King did not want to care for his child, but he was not evil, he was just important. The new Queen was desirable and wanted to do other things than care for a child, which proves that she was evil.

Knowing that his Evil Queen wanted to do these other things, the King, who was important but not stupid, asked a sorcerer to make a magic mirror. "Ensorcell it so it will talk to her every day," he commanded, "but make it so it can never tell her truths, it can only lie."

The Sorcerer did as the King commanded and after their wedding the King gave the magic mirror to the Evil Queen.

"You are my wife and my Queen," he said, "you are too busy caring for me and my child to talk to any of the women at my court and too beautiful to talk to the men, so I am giving you this mirror. You must sit in front of it every day and talk to it about what you want and how you feel". He had his servants hang it on the wall in her room and returned to his wars and his money.

Even Evil Queens can get lonely, so she spent many hours in front of the mirror that lied to her, talking to it about all the other things she wanted to do and the child she did not want to care for. But the mirror that lied to her was not there to listen or care for her. Its only purpose was to lie.

"You are still young and beautiful," it said, "You cannot be anything else. You earn your place in the world with your beauty and the world wants nothing else from you. Accept this and you will be happy. You must also teach these lessons to Little Snow White. Even you, so evil that you do not want children, are required to ensure that little girls are good and sweet and obedient."

For many years, the Evil Queen had no one to talk to but the mirror that lied to her, and so she came to trust it and believed its lies were truth. When Little Snow White was seven years old, the mirror that lied to her told the Evil Queen the child she did not want was becoming a danger to her.

"Little Snow White is growing up and you are growing older," it said, "Look how beautiful she is becoming! Look how sweet and graceful and obedient she is! Soon she will take your place as the King's most beautiful possession and then you will have no place in the world."

The Evil Queen was terrified. "What can I do?" she asked the mirror that lied to her, "How can I save myself?"

"There is only space for one beautiful woman here and you must keep it for yourself," replied the mirror that lied to her, "You must have Snow White killed."

"Kill her? She's only a child! Surely that would be too evil even for me," cried the Evil Queen. She ran from the mirror that lied to her and roamed the castle, wishing she could be something other than beautiful and evil and in danger.

The Evil Queen begged and pleaded with the mirror that lied to her, but every day it told her she had to kill Little Snow White or lose her own place in the world.

Eventually, the Evil Queen called one of the King's hunters to her and ordered him to kill little Snow White. The hunter was a Good Man who did not know he was responsible for his own choices. He agreed to take Little Snow White to the woods and kill her, as any Good Man would do.

Little Snow White was sweet and kind and obedient, so she made no objection to being taken off to the silent forest by the Good Man who was going to kill her.

When a Good Man kills a child in a fairy tale, it needs to happen in a dark forest, so the Good Man took Little Snow White to the deepest, darkest heart of the forest, drew his knife and prepared to plunge it into Little Snow White's chest. Little Snow White was too unselfish to fight for her life, all she could do was cry and beg.

The Good Man was touched by her willingness to die for her role as a passive victim in her own story and decided he would not stab her through the heart. <u>"Run away, then, you poor child,"</u> he said. <u>"The wild beasts will soon devour you."</u> And <u>it seemed as if a stone had been rolled from his heart since he no longer needed to kill her.</u> Such a relief for the Good Man, that he only had to leave a little child to a lonely, terrifying death in the forest rather than kill her with his own hands.

Little Snow White obediently ran away through the deepest darkest heart of the forest. She ran and ran and ran but she did not know which direction to take and could not find her way back to the father who was too busy to care for her or the stepmother who had been taught to fear and hate her.

Eventually she found a little cottage and inside was a kitchen, a table with seven chairs and a room with seven beds. Exhausted and starving, she ate some food from the kitchen, drank some wine from a glass and fell asleep on one of the beds.

While she slept, the owners of the cottage arrived home. They were miners who spent the daylight hours delving under the mountain for ore that made the kingdom rich. The seven miners could not afford a cottage each, so they all shared the one. Spending all their days away from the sun making rich men richer had stunted their growth and maimed their bodies, which makes them the perfect comic relief for a fairy tale about murdering children.

The seven miners saw Little Snow White asleep in one of the beds, all tear-stained, scratched and dirty. "Look!" they cried, "a traumatised child! We had best not wake her or ask how she came to be here. We are only men and cannot be expected to care for a child. We'll go to sleep and wait to see what happens in the morning."

The next day Little Snow White woke up and was amazed to find the seven miners standing over her. She told them about the Evil Queen who was so afraid of youth that she'd asked a Good Man to kill a little girl, and the Good Man who was relieved he only had to leave her to die, and the King who was too busy to care for his daughter.

"Never mind all that," said the miners, "you're here now and we don't need to worry about what happened to bring you here. <u>If you will take care of our house, cook, make the beds, wash, sew, and knit, and if you will keep everything neat and clean, you can stay with us and you shall want for nothing.</u>"

The miners were delighted to have a little girl to do all the things men should not have to do and went cheerfully back to work in the mines while Little Snow White did all the things only women and little girls should do. While they were gone, she made friends with the birds and animals of the forest and sang happy songs about how wonderful it is to do unpaid work for men who work for money.

Meanwhile, the Evil Queen, believing the Good Man had killed Little Snow White, was back at her husband's castle, trying to keep her place in the world. The mirror that lied to her told her she could not hope to do so if she continued to grow older. "You are not beautiful anymore," said the mirror that lied to her. "You have no purpose now. All that is left to you is to be a cautionary tale for little girls, a warning to never grow old lest men despise you and the world ignore you."

"But why?" the Evil Queen cried, "Why can't I be something more than hateful and ugly?"

"You are a woman," replied the mirror that lied to her, "you're old and you have no children, what else is there for you to be?"

The Evil Queen bowed her head and cried because she knew the mirror that lied to her was telling the truth.

"By the way," it added, "Little Snow White is still alive. She has all the youth and beauty that used to be yours. Tear her down and maybe, just maybe, you will build yourself up again."

The Evil Queen who believed she was too old to be beautiful disguised herself as an old woman and went out to search for Snow White.

Many weary hours later, she found the little cottage where Little Snow White spent her days alone, cooking, cleaning, sewing, and knitting for men who did not need to do women's work now she was there.

The Evil Queen gave Little Snow White a poisoned apple. The miners had forgotten to teach Little Snow White to fear and hate old women, so she ate the poisonous apple and fell to the ground, unconscious.

"Finally," said the Evil Queen, "I have removed the threat of youth and beauty. I am safe again." She left Little Snow White on the floor and went back to the castle to ask the mirror that lied to her if her beauty was still enough to make her matter to the world.

When the seven miners came back to the little cottage, they found Little Snow White lying on the floor, pale and cold, and believed she was dead. Instead of burying her, they encased her in a glass casket because beautiful girls don't need to be alive for men to gaze at them. They wrote her name on it in golden letters and, of course, also wrote that she was a king's daughter. It's important, even for dead girls, that they belong to powerful men.

One day a Handsome Prince came riding through the woods. He saw the glass casket and Little Snow White lying cold and still inside it. He demanded that the seven miners give it to him because they were only miners and he was a Prince, and miners should never have beautiful things that are denied to Princes.

"Let me have it as a gift, for I cannot live without seeing Snow White. I will honour and prize her as my dearest possession," he told them.

The seven miners understood that even dead, beautiful girls always belong to princes, so they gave the casket and Little Snow White to him. He had his servant carry it, but they were clumsy, as servants of the rich so often are, and when they jolted the casket enough that a piece of poisoned apple fell out of Little Snow White's throat, she woke up.

"Where am I?" she asked, "What happened to me?"

"That doesn't matter," said the Handsome Prince joyfully to the little girl he had thought was dead, "I love you more than everything in the world; come with me to my father's palace, you shall be my wife."

Even though the Evil Queen had been taught to hate her and the Good Man had tried to kill her, and the seven miners had tried to enslave her, and the busy King had succeeded in ignoring her, Little Snow White was still a good obedient girl, so she agreed to marry the Handsome Prince who loved her because she was beautiful and dead and a child. Their wedding was held with great show and splendour, which all worthily passive girls deserve.

The Evil Queen was invited too and because she was a woman who got old and wanted things, she was not allowed to have choices, so she went to their wedding.

After the wedding, for no particular reason, all the men whose violence was erased from Little Snow White's story put iron dancing slippers in a fire. Once they were burning brightly, they took the slippers to the Evil Queen with tongs and <u>she was forced to put on the red-hot shoes and dance until she dropped down dead</u>. The men laughed and clapped and cheered and said it was the best wedding they had ever seen.

No one lived happily ever after, except the Handsome Prince, who never had reason to be anything but happy.

The End

Cinderella

In the Grimm Brothers' version of Cinderella (quotes from their story are underlined), her mother dies in the first sentence and by the end of the first paragraph has been replaced by an evil stepmother. Their Cinderella is an innocent, beautiful girl who suffers at the hands of a wicked older woman and bad-tempered, avaricious stepsisters. They mock her and force her to do all the unpaid labour of running a large household. Even the name her mother gave her is erased and replaced with a sneer: she always looked dusty and dirty, they called her Cinderella.

Her only option for escape comes when the King holds a three-day festival to which all the beautiful young girls in the country were invited, in order that his son might choose himself a bride.

Cinderella, who has no friends or family other than her neglectful father and cruel step-family, goes to her mother's grave to ask for help. There is no fairy godmother, but magic birds bring her beautiful dresses that transform her from a dirty servant into a beautiful woman. This transformation was as much about class as it was about beauty. Poverty was dirty, shameful, and difficult to escape. Rich gowns appearing by magic were Cinderella's passport to wealth because not even a beautiful and pure young girl could find a Handsome Prince if she remained poor.

She goes to the festival, the Handsome Prince falls instantly in love with her, and will not let her dance with anyone else. When she wants to leave, he says, "<u>I will go with you and bear you company,</u>" for he wished <u>to see to whom the beautiful maiden belonged.</u>

The first two nights of the festival she dances with him and then runs away. On the last night he is determined to find her despite her obvious wishes (clearly, she's just playing hard to get). He pours sticky pitch on the steps, and she leaves a shoe stuck to it as she escapes. The Handsome Prince then makes all the women in the town try on the shoe because his bride must prove her perfection and he cannot recognise Cinderella simply by looking at her.

At their mother's bidding, Cinderella's stepsisters take a knife and cut off their toes and heels to fit their big feet into the cast-off shoe. Disgusted by their blood, the Handsome Prince rejects them. He asks Cinderella's father if he has any other daughters, and the father replies, "<u>There is still a little stunted kitchen-wench which my late wife left behind, but she cannot possibly be the bride.</u>"

Despite her father's denial that she is his daughter or a suitable bride for a Prince, the shoe fits and the Handsome Prince declares that he has found his <u>true bride</u>. At the wedding, the magic birds tear out the stepsisters' eyes and the story ends.

I couldn't stick to this original plot, where a pure young girl is rescued from drudgery and the jealousy of other women by being so pretty and passive that even Handsome Prince will marry her. So, I gave her Disney's Fairy Godmother, the traditional three wishes, and a feminist's desire to make the world a better place…

Once upon a time there was a very rich man. As is the habit of rich men, he had a beautiful wife. And he also had a daughter. When the daughter was almost grown, the wife became sick and feeling that her end was near, she called her daughter to her and said, "Dear child, be good and pious, and then the good God will always protect you, and I will look down on you from heaven and be near you." Then she closed her eyes and died, as mothers always do in fairy tales.

The girl was grief stricken. Every day she went to her mother's grave and lay down on it to cry. She did her best to be good and pious, but the rich man who was her father did not notice her and the God her mother said was good did not protect her.

Even rich men cannot stand to be alone, so he found another beautiful woman and she agreed to be his wife because she had two daughter and no choices. The rich man knew that four women in his house, even if they have no choices of their own, can be powerful if they band together, so taught his new wife and stepdaughters to disdain his oldest child.

He took all the nice clothes and pretty things from the oldest daughter and gave them to his stepdaughters, making sure they knew he could do the same to them if they displeased him. He mocked and bullied the daughter of his first wife and rewarded the second wife and her daughter when they did the same. The new wife and her daughters, who had no choices, sadly colluded in his abuse.

The oldest daughter <u>had to do hard work from morning till night, get up before daybreak, carry water, light fires, cook and wash. Besides this, the sisters did her every imaginable injury.</u> At night she slept on the floor in front of the kitchen fire. Her father laughed about the ash stains and cinder burns on her skin and told everyone to call her Cinderella. Sad and scared, the new wife and stepdaughters obeyed him and prayed every night that he would not turn his rage upon them.

On her eighteenth birthday Cinderella returned to her mother's grave and lay down to cry again. "I miss you so much," she sobbed. "I tried to do what you said, I tried to be good and pious, I waited for God to protect me. Where is God? Where are you? How can I escape this horrible man who is supposed to love me and care for me? Why can't my stepmother love me? I wish, oh how I wish everything could be different."

Great heaving sobs hurt her body and made her head ache but no matter how much she cried and prayed and wished, God did not answer, and her mother was still dead.

Cinderella lay on the grave until her sobbing slowly eased and the exhausted hopelessness that comes after crying with no relief set in. "What do I do now?" she said despairingly.

"Well, you should start by wiping all the snot off your face," answered a clear voice above her. Cinderella sat up with a start and stared in wonder at the fairy sitting on her mother's gravestone.

"Who are you?" she asked in amazement.

"I'm your fairy godmother, of course" answered the fairy. "Abused girls who lie sobbing on their mother's grave are usually left to cry alone, but this is a fairy tale, so, here I am. Now, get up, you're a mess. Let's get you cleaned up and we'll talk about what I can do for you."

The Fairy Godmother bounced down from her perch on the gravestone and helped Cinderella to her feet. She brushed the dirt from her clothes, wiped her face clean and gave her a hug.

"There, that's a bit better. Now, let's go somewhere a bit warmer. We're not going to solve anything standing in a graveyard." She put her arm around Cinderella, waved her wand, and suddenly the two of them were sitting on comfortable chairs in a warm room.

"Tea?" she asked. Cinderella nodded, still too befuddled to speak and watched with wide eyes as the Fairy Godmother waved her wand again and poured two cups from the teapot that winked into being on the table.

"Ok, now, let's get you sorted. This is a fairy tale, so get comfortable with suspending disbelief. I'm here to grant you three wishes. Anything you want. Silk dresses? Everlasting beauty? Drop three dress sizes in under a minute? I can give you all the things that make women happy."

Cinderella sipped her tea and suspended her disbelief. "Anything? Anything at all?"

"Yep, and if you word it right, you can get yourself a whole room full of shoes on one wish. It's all about clarity. You can't ask for something unless you can articulate it properly, so take a minute to think about how you word it."

"What if I want something really special?"

"Hah! You want love? A Handsome Prince to whisk you away from all of this and live happily ever after in a great big castle? Easy! I've been doing that for centuries."

Cinderella snorted. "A Handsome Prince? Another man who's going to want me to wash his clothes and clean his mess and shore up his ego. What a waste of a wish. No, I want something much better than that."

The Fairy Godmother grinned. "Something better than a Handsome Prince? The world is full of such things, all to be had for the wishing of them. What is it you want?" She twirled her wand merrily.

Cinderella sat up straighter in her chair. "My name is not Cinderella. My father called me that when I was burned by the cinders where he made me sleep, but it's not my name. My mother called me Anvika."

The Fairy Godmother lowered her wand and looked disgusted. "I'm sorry, Anvika. Your father sounds like a right cunt. And if we're having names like we're actual people instead of clichés, my name is Joan."

"Joan the fairy godmother? Seriously?" Joan nodded and grinned happily.

"Alright then," Anvika took a firm grip on her suspended disbelief and ploughed on. "So, Joan, if I asked, you could give me world peace?"

"Oh, yes. We might have put a whole lot of expectations on your wishes but there's no limits. Anything you want."

Anvika nodded thoughtfully. "Well, we definitely could do with some peace, but as you say, it's all in how you word it, isn't it?"

"Yeah, that's always the tricky bit. I mean, you could wish for world peace, but what happens to the world after you die? Or you could wish that everyone in the world had no hands so they could never shoot a gun again, but it wouldn't take long before someone worked out how to do voice activated shooting and nothing would really change. Words matter. Be careful what you wish for."

They sat quietly for a while, the abused girl and the Fairy Godmother who were actually people with names and complex lives. Anvika frowned as she thought her way through the tangle of things she wanted. She pictured her father, so afraid of women that he had to force them to hate each other. Her stepmother who had no choices and her stepsisters who were too scared to be kind. She remembered her mother, who loved her so much and how as she lay dying all she could do was cling to the belief that being good and believing in God would be enough to keep her daughter safe.

"It's all a bit fucked, isn't it?" she said to Joan.

"It is indeed," Joan replied, because she was a magical Fairy Godmother and knew what Anvika was thinking without being told.

"Alright, I think I've got it." Anvika ran through the wishes in her head one last time, adjusting the wording and thinking through the consequences.

Joan picked up her wand and waited.

"I wish every girl and woman in the world had the same access to wealth that men have always had."

"Done!" Joan waved her wand.

"I wish every girl and woman in the world always had the same access to power that men have always had."

"Done!" Joan waved her wand again.

"I wish that no man or boy ever could or ever will be able to use violence of any kind against any person."

"And done!" Joan waved her wand a final time and "Oh, this is going to be fucking hilarious!" She lay back in her chair and laughed until she cried.

Anvika laughed too. "Can we go see what's happening?" she asked eagerly. "Do you think it will be very different?"

Joan was still laughing. "Different? It's going to be utterly unrecognisable. Come on, let's go have a look."

She took Anvika 's hand and raced out with her to look at a world where men had the same power and wealth as women and could never ever be violent.

They walked through Anvika's village. It was night but the streets were full of people. Women were everywhere. Walking at night on their own, striding along confidently past men who did not look at them or call out to them or interrupt them. Children played happy night-time games on the street and ran to safe homes to be greeted by mothers who had birthed them by choice and could afford to feed them well and care for them properly. Men stood in groups, looking pleadingly at each other but saying very little.

Anvika watched the men as they stood uneasily together. "Will they be ok?" she asked.

Joan rolled her eyes. "Of course they will. It will take them a bit of time, but they'll get used to it. They're just feeling a bit lost right now. They don't know how to live in a world without their power and wealth and violence, but they'll work it out and be much happier for it."

A group of little boys ran past them, shouting and laughing as they chased each other. One fell down and the others stopped to pick him up and make sure he wasn't hurt. "See?" Joan said as they watched the boys hug the one who fell, "They'll be fine. Do you want to go home and see your father?"

"Um, I guess so." Anvika said nervously.

They kept walking down the busy street. Shops were open everywhere, wide open windows displaying beautifully arranged food and warm, comfortable clothes with lots of pockets. A little girl ran past and snatched an apple from a stall. A woman ran after her with a broom and smacked it out of her hands. "Little thief," she cried, "How dare you?" and she whacked the little girl with the broom.

"Oh," said Anvika, "I didn't think of that."

"I know," Joan replied. "Women are not all lovely angels, born only to nurture and care. And what about the queers? Didn't think about them at all did you?"

"Oh, but… I mean… I'm sorry…" stammered Anvika.

"Too late now. And don't apologise to me hoping for absolution. What do you think I am? Some plot device written in to cover up your straight lady bias? Pfft. Suck it up princess. You've had your wishes and now you'll have to live with the consequences. Come on, we're nearly there."

They arrived at Anvika's father's house. It was still large and comfortable, but it had lost the lustre of wealth it used to have. Anvika hung back, thinking of the apple seller and wondering what her stepmother and stepsisters would do when she came home.

"This is what happens when you have choices," Joan told her. "There are always consequences. You can't hide from them. Go on. It's time to see what your wishing has done for you."

She opened the door and dragged Anvika through.

The stepmother was standing in the hallways surrounded by boxes. She looked up as Anvika was thrust through the door and frowned.

"Where have you been?" she snapped.

"Just out. I'm sorry." Anvika 's heart sank. Her wishes had changed the world, but her home was no different.

"No, it's ok. Don't apologise." The stepmother looked around at all the boxes. "Packing always drives me crazy but I wanted to see you before we leave."

"You… I… what? Where are you going?"

"Well I'm leaving of course! Your father is awful, no woman in her right mind would stay with him. I have choices now, and I choose to be anywhere but here with him."

"I... Oh, yes..." Anvika looked at the woman she wanted so much to love her and realised her wishes had come true, but they had not given her what she wanted.

The Stepmother came and gently put her hand on Anvika's face. "I know I was not good to you. I couldn't love you or care for you as you wanted when I had no choices and it's too late now. I have to leave, and I didn't ever choose you, so I will not take you with me. Will you be ok on your own?"

"I think so," Anvika said cautiously.

"Yes, I think so too. I know it would be easier for you if you had someone to guide you, but I have my own daughters to care for and my own life to live. I wish you well Cinderella, I really do, but I choose to not be responsible for you."

She patted Anvika's cheek and hurried away, not hearing the wistful "Cinderella was never my name" that followed her.

Anvika turned and saw Joan watching from the shadows. "Do you regret your wishes now? You could have wished that she would love you as her own daughter for the rest of her life."

Before she could answer, her two stepsisters came running down the stairs, carrying bags of clothes. They stopped and exchanged glances as they saw Anvika standing in the hallway.

Anvika waited. The stepsisters walked slowly down the remaining stairs to the hall and put the bags with the pile of boxes next to the door.

"Some of those are mine," she said.

The older stepsister stepped forward. "I know, but some of them are ours too. We had nothing when we came here, you know. Your father gave us your things and he bought us new things to reward us for hating you. All of them are tainted."

She looked at her sister. "What do you think? Should we burn them all and start again?"

The younger stepsister looked alarmed. "Really? Why? We all paid a high price for these things and some of them are lovely. I don't want to lose them all."

They turned to Anvika.

"I don't care," she said, suddenly exhausted by everything that had happened that day. "Take what you want, leave what you don't. You two are not my problem anymore." She turned away and started up the stairs to find her father. As she walked past them, she heard a soft whisper, "We're so sorry, Cinderella."

"My name was never Cinderella," she said without turning her head and continued up the stairs.

She found her father sitting in the bedroom he used to share with Anvika 's mother and then with the new wife. He was watching silently as the new wife was flinging the last of her belongings into a suitcase.

"I only married you because I had no choices," the new wife said to him as she zipped up her suitcase. "You were not a man any woman would choose. Now that women do not need your power or wealth, what are you going to offer a woman that she would choose you and then choose to stay with you?"

Anvika 's father searched for words that were not violent and things that were not power or money, but all he had to offer was silence.

"Exactly!" The stepmother picked up her suitcase, nodded to Anvika and swept out the door.

Anvika walked over and closed the doors to the empty closet. She turned and looked at her father, waiting for him to say something.

At last he spoke. "I am sorry," he said with tears in his eyes. "I never learned how to be anything other than what I was. I wanted to love you, but I was too scared. What if you left me? What if she rejected me? What would I do?"

Anvika considered his words. "I understand, I think," she said, "but you had choices, and this is what you chose. Now you get to live with the consequences of the things you chose and the wishes I made."

She walked away from him, down the stairs, past the pile of bags and boxes, past Joan the Fairy Godmother and out into the world where women were safe and men were not violent.

They did not all live happily ever after, but they did have very interesting lives.

The End

Sleeping Beauty

Sleeping Beauty is perhaps the least interesting of all the princess stories. In the Grimm Brother's version, the baby princess is cursed with death by an evil old "Wise Woman" as vengeance for being ignored, because all old women are evil, especially the ones who will not be ignored. The curse is softened by a less evil Wise Woman who decrees that instead of dying, the princess will sleep for a hundred years. Despite all the King's attempts to avert her fate, the princess succumbs to the curse and the entire castle falls into an enchanted sleep. Just as the prescribed hundred years ends, a Handsome Prince arrives and sexually assaults the Princess while she's unconscious. She wakes up, falls in love with the Handsome Prince, and they live happily ever after.

Perhaps the reason this story is so simple is because the Grimm Brothers had to excise so many details from the original story. Without all the rape and attempted cannibalism, there wasn't much plot left (more details about the original story are in the first chapter if you're curious).

I couldn't write a woman sleeping through her own story, and I definitely couldn't re-write the original (I have no interest in morality tales about rape) so I had to find a new story. Sleeping Beauty is one of the few fairy tale princesses whose mother isn't killed off in the first paragraph. She's also the only one who interacts with an older woman who isn't completely evil. It's not much, but it gave me a place to start.

A few of these retellings went to some dark places (looking at you, Beauty and the Beast) and I didn't want the whole book to be about the worst things that men do to women. This was my chance to have some fun - and I did.

Also, just so you know, Gattara means "cat lady", Xanthippe was Socrates' wife, she was so vilified that her name later became synonymous with bitter, nagging wives, and Carson is a friend of mine. I find things like this funny, but it's ok if you don't.

Once upon a time there was a King, but he was not in the least bit interesting, so we won't mention him again.

A long time ago in a land far away, there was much rejoicing when a woman called Gattara gave birth to a big, strong baby girl. Gattara was the wisest of the Wise Women, the council of elders who governed the land. The people were not rejoicing because the baby would inherit the Wise Woman mantle (that's a title you have to earn goddamnit, you don't just get born into it) but because her people were so delighted that she and the baby had survived the dangers of childbirth, and look, that's always something to celebrate. Who doesn't love a party?

Gattara named her daughter Talia, in the hope that her daughter could reclaim the name given to some old dude's fantasy about women who wake up delighted to find they've been raped.

Gattara, as was incumbent on the wisest of Wise Women, was a teacher at the local children's academy. She taught the most important subjects, critical thinking, communication, and science. Old Witch Carson (given this special title of respect and eminence for her contributions to the fields of Morris dancing and safe, affordable abortion) taught healthcare, pharmacology, and dance. Wise Woman Xanthippe taught maths, history, military tactics, and self-defence. It was all a bit irritatingly earnest and idealistic, but, honestly, what did you expect from a feminist fairy tale?

Talia grew from a big strong baby into a sturdy toddler, full of curiosity and adventurous spirit. She joined the Children's Academy and learned how to play and share, to resolve conflict with others and within herself. As she grew, she absorbed all the lessons on the functions of government and understood the social contract between people who are chosen to rule and people who choose how they are ruled. She read treatises on the history of empires so she could learn from the mistakes of the past, and dissertations on ethics and critical thinking so she could choose not to recreate them. She learned to ride a horse, swim a river, and tend to wounds. By the time she reached adulthood, she had been taught to understand the mechanics of sex, gender, periods, nocturnal emissions, and the physiology of orgasm. And before this gets any more cloying, it's time to move the story along.

Late one summer afternoon, not long after Talia's eighteenth birthday, tired out after a vigorous fencing lesson with Wise Woman Xanthippe, she was taking a nap next to the rose garden at the Children's Academy.

In a typical fairy tale coincidence, just as Talia fell asleep, a Handsome Prince rode past the Academy and decided, for no particular reason, to climb the walls and have a wander through a building he had no right to enter.

"Ow, ow, ow," said the Handsome Prince, as he manfully ignored the sweeping pathway and fought his way through the thorny rose bushes. He swung his mighty sword at the roses and with doughty strokes, beheaded a particularly sweet-smelling yellow rose. He flexed his bare arms in case someone was watching and tried to mask his squeaks of pain with rugged grunts. Finally, he won his intrepid battle with the flowers and burst out onto the lawn where Talia lay sleeping.

"Oh, a fair maiden!" the Handsome Prince cried, gazing at the sleeping Talia. "How hotly the blood courses through my veins in contemplation of so many charms. I shall carry her off to my bed and there I shall gather the first fruits of love!"

He bent over Talia and tried to sweep her up in his arms.

"What in the name of arse-guzzling fuck are you doing?" yelled Talia as she woke up, shoved the Handsome Prince's hands off her waist and jumped to her feet.

The Handsome Prince beamed at her. "Fair maiden, you need fear no more. I have come to rescue you!" he proclaimed proudly, reaching out a gleaming arm towards her.

"Touch me again and I will fucking end you, cunt," snapped Talia.

The Handsome Prince's wide smile dropped, and he looked doubtfully at Talia's rangy frame and close-cropped hair. "You are a fair maiden, aren't you? A hidden princess in need of rescue?" He thoughtfully flexed his biceps and waited for her admiring gasp.

"Princess of my wide white arse," Talia snorted. "What is wrong with you? Is this how you spend your afternoons? Chopping up rose bushes and grabbing at any sleeping woman you find? Why hasn't anyone nailed a bucket on your head?"

As Talia was looking around the garden in search of a bucket, Xanthippe, Gattara and Old Witch Carson arrived to investigate the shouting, followed by all the students of the Academy.

Xanthippe looked at the confused and muscular Handsome Prince, still dripping blood from his battle with the rose bushes and started to laugh. "Are we starting clown classes!" she asked and poked Gattara in the ribs, "Good move. We're all getting a bit too stuffy and serious, a bit of old fashioned slapstick is exactly what this place needs."

The Handsome Prince stared at her in horror. "Old… woman..? Are you a woman? You look like a man … those breeches, that hair…but… What are you?"

Xanthippe laughed even harder. "Why, little man? Are you looking for a date?" She leered at him and waggled her tongue.

"Am I… what… You……you…" the Handsome Prince picked up his sword and advanced on Xanthippe.

"Put that thing down before I hurt you with it," barked Talia, and expertly flipped the sword from the Handsome Prince's hand. She turned to Gattara. "Mama, I have no idea why this preening little milksop is here or why he made such a mess of the garden. Maybe he's just scared of roses. But I will not let him put his hands on me. I don't care how much flower related trauma he's carrying." She glared at the Handsome Prince and tightened her grip on his sword.

Gattara nodded and said calmly, "Indeed my daughter, you could well have wreaked a bloody vengeance upon him. He is fortunate that you refrained."

The Handsome Prince looked indignant and rippled more muscle at her. "What do you mean? I did nothing wrong! She was lying on the ground, displaying all her…"

Old Witch Carson's laughter was as loud as Xanthippe's. "You want us to blame Talia, little peacock? Did your brain fall out in the rose garden? Why would anyone believe such nonsense?"

"Why? Why would they not believe me? I am a man and a prince! A handsome one at that," said the Handsome Prince. "Look at my muscles and my manly chin!" He thrust his chin out at Xanthippe and glared threateningly.

Xanthippe doubled over, wailing in mirth. "Believe him! Him! That mewling mooncalf! Ahahahaha. That's the funniest thing I've heard since the King tried to explain which hole babies come out of."

Xanthippe and Old Witch Carson leaned against each other and laughed 'til they cried. The indignant look fought a brief battle with a puzzled frown for possession of the Handsome Prince's face, then gave up and fled the field.

He turned back to the calm, dignified Gattara and said, "I do not understand these cackling harridans. You, a good and queenly woman, you will listen to me and give me the maiden for my wife, so she can live happily ever after managing all my affairs and raising my children."

"No," Gattara replied calmly and turned to her daughter.

"Talia, what do you want to do with this man who put his hands on you?"

The Handsome Prince's face found its beam again, and he strode confidently forward, "My beautiful bride!"

Talia bared her teeth at him. "I'd sooner marry a syphilitic ferret. Step back, fuckboy." She turned to her mother and smiled, "All I want from him, Mama, is an apology. I think he owes me that much."

The delighted beam dropped off the Handsome Prince's face, never to appear again. Desperately trying ignore more howls of laughter from Xanthippe and Old Witch Carson, he turned back to Gattara. "This is a terrible place! The garden is a mess, and the women are all liars. It's time for me to leave."

Gattara quickly stepped in front of him. "No. You will not leave here until you have told Talia the truth of what you intended when you laid hands on her and expressed your true remorse for the choices you made. We will not exact any further punishment of you, but you will do at least that much for her."

"Remorse? For what? For attempting to rescue her from this coven of witches? For offering to save her life and glorify her future? You crazy old shrew, let me pass!"

The Handsome Prince tried to push Gattara aside and was promptly restrained by the still snickering Xanthippe and Old Witch Carson. "Hold up there, son," said Xanthippe, "You've got a job to do before you scurry off."

Old Witch Carson wiped her eyes. "It's simple enough for a big strong lad like you. Courageous truth and a manly apology. How hard could it be?" Her lips still twitching, she patted the Handsome Prince on the head. "Get it out, boy. You'll feel much better afterwards and then you can be on your way."

The Handsome Prince struggled but could not free himself from their grip.

Gattara spoke again. "The choice is yours, as it was when you came here. Truth and remorse will set you free. Until then you will stay in the rose garden you abused so wantonly."

She gave quick instructions to the gathered students, and within a very short time they had constructed a fence around the rose garden and hung a huge bell over the gate.

"We do not have any more time to waste on you," Gattara told the Handsome Prince. "When you are ready to give Talia the truth and remorse you owe her, ring the bell and we will all come to bear witness. Until then, you can eat the food that grows here and drink the water that flows her, but nothing else will be given to you or taken from you until you give Talia her restitution."

Old Witch Carson grinned toothily at the Handsome Prince and shoved him through the gate. Xanthippe locked it behind him, linked arms with Talia, and walked off whistling.

For many years the Handsome Prince believed that all the people of the land told their children about the legend of the Handsome Prince who slept behind the wall of climbing roses, and he waited for a beautiful, unselfish princess to rescue him from truth and remorse. But everyone was busy doing interesting things and they forgot all about the Handsome Prince.

He sat in the garden behind his prison of lies until he grew old and died and was eaten by worms and birds.

No one noticed.

The End

The Little Mermaid

The Little Mermaid was religious allegory written by Hans Christian Anderson. It's about the rewards in the afterlife for women who give uncomplaining love and silence to men who treat them badly. The Little Mermaid is a child by today's standards, but she is a cypher for the pain women and girls must willingly embrace for conformity.

In the original story, the Little Mermaid falls in love with the Handsome Prince and strikes a deal with an evil and ugly Sea Witch (because all the wicked witches in fairy tales are ugly or old or both). The Sea Witch offers her a magic potion that will give her legs but demands three things in return: every step she takes on land will feel like stepping on knives, she must let the Sea Witch cut out her tongue, and if the Handsome

Prince marries someone else, the Little Mermaid will die, soulless and alone.

She is so desperate to live in the world above the sea with her Handsome Prince that she agrees to the deal. Without her voice, however, she cannot tell him the sacrifices she has made for him and so he doesn't know she is unselfish enough to be his princess. Instead, he falls in love with a girl who has not sacrificed her voice to win his love and decides to marry her.

The Little Mermaid's sisters come to tell her they have traded their hair to the Sea Witch for a cure. If she stabs the Handsome Prince through the heart on his wedding day and pours his blood onto her legs, her fish tail will come back, and she can live again as a mermaid. The Little Mermaid decides the Handsome Prince's life is worth more than her own and throws herself into the sea. As she dies, angels come to her and say that because she sacrificed her life for the Handsome Prince, she has the chance to become an ethereal being and if she devotes herself to doing good but invisible deeds for humans for 300 years, she will be allowed to go to heaven. They tell her that whenever she sees a good child who is <u>the joy of his parents and deserves</u>

their love, the 300 years will be reduced by a day, but every naughty or wicked child she sees will add a day to her sentence, and the story ends. Disney, in addition to songs and talking sea creatures, added a happy ending and took out the blood and mutilation.

I didn't want to erase the mermaid's bad choices, we all make them and there's usually growth in that. But I couldn't perpetuate the 'women are evil when they get old' trope or the myth of self-abnegation as a virtue, so I wrote a different ending. Again, quotes from the original story are underlined.

Once upon a time there was a Little Mermaid princess who had no name. She lived in a beautiful underwater kingdom with her father, the King, her grandmother, and her five older sisters. The Little Mermaid's mother died when she was a baby because mothers have no role in fairy tales for children.

The King sent each of his daughters to the surface on her fifteenth birthday so she could see the people who lived on land. When she returned, he asked each daughter to tell her sisters what she had seen of the lives they could never have.

The King's youngest daughter had no name, she was just the Little Mermaid. She loved listening to the exciting stories of the land where people had legs instead of a tail; where they drank and danced and killed each other. She dreamed of playing with trees and talking to flowers and fighting with swords.

Finally, it was her turn. Her sisters helped brush her hair and polish her scales. Laughing and calling farewells, they swam with her to the borders of their father's kingdom.

The Little Mermaid swam to the surface alone. She breathed air, saw stars, and heard birds for the first time. She laughed and cried and laughed again.

Not far from where she swam with her laughter and tears, a ship was floating. There were lights along the rails and masts, and beautiful people dancing on the decks. Below deck, where she could not see, the servants worked and the soldiers waited.

"How lovely they are," the Little Mermaid said, "how joyful and free!"

She swam closer and saw, at the centre of the dancers, a Handsome Prince.

The Little Mermaid was mesmerised. "Look how they all gather around him and wait for him to speak," she said to herself, "he must be very good and wise for them to love him so." She watched for hours as the Handsome Prince talked and the pretty girls giggled, and the handsome men guffawed.

The Little Mermaid swam around and around the ship, falling more and more in love with the Handsome Prince. So full of love was she that she didn't notice the storm coming in until it broke, sending crashing waves and thundering winds to toss the ship around and break it all apart.

Even the Little Mermaid was shocked by the violence of the storm. The people from the land were crushed and broken by the waves and the wind. She was small and not very strong, but she swam mightily, ignoring the bruises and tears on her body as she searched for the Handsome Prince, who she loved even though she did not know him.

Finally, after everyone else had drowned, she found him. Just as he was losing consciousness, she grabbed him and held his exhausted body against her chest all night, shielding him from waves and the tossing pieces of wood. As the sun came up, the storm passed and the weary Little Mermaid still floated in the sea, holding the unconscious Handsome Prince above water, keeping him alive.

Eventually they drifted close to land. Crying with exhaustion, the Little Mermaid dragged him onto land. She could not stay with him, but she forced her strong tail through the sand to lie him down above the water's edge. Gasping in pain and relief she returned to the ocean and rested on a rocky outcrop near the beach. She watched anxiously as the Handsome Prince lay unmoving in the sun. Was it too late? Had all her efforts to save him been in vain? She couldn't tell and couldn't return to land to see if he still lived. She cried and cried, cursing her mermaid's tail that could never walk on land.

As she cried and watched and cursed, a Beautiful Girl came to the beach and saw the Handsome Prince's body. The Beautiful Girl, who also was a thing without a name, cried out in alarm and ran to the Handsome Prince's aid.

The Handsome Prince opened his eyes and vomited sea water all over the Beautiful Girl's dress. The Beautiful Girl laughed with relief that he was alive and smiled prettily as he squeezed her waist and told her how strongly he had swum to escape the sinking ship and raging storm. They turned away from the sea and did not see the Little Mermaid, crying and watching on the rocks behind them.

The Handsome Prince led the Beautiful Girl away from the sea and into a palace by the water's edge. The Little Mermaid, who had suffered so much to save his life, fell into an exhausted sleep on the rocks. She slept until sunset and when she woke there was no one left on the beach. She slid down from the rocks and slowly returned to her father's kingdom.

Her grandmother and sisters greeted her at the gates. "You were gone so long!" they cried, "We were so worried about you. What happened? Why are you all cut and bruised?" The Little Mermaid did not tell them about falling in love with the Handsome Prince she did not know. She did not tell them that he didn't know how she had suffered to save him and lost him to a Beautiful Girl with human legs. Her father, the King, had been too busy to teach her about shame and how it is always held in secret by people who have no right to it.

For months the Little Mermaid stayed in her sea garden with her secret shame and her secret love and waited for her body to heal from the wounds she bore from saving the Handsome Prince's life. When her had recovered, she swam back to the beach where she had saved and lost her Prince. Sometimes she heard the fishermen talking about the taxes he raised and the laws he broke. The Little Mermaid didn't know about taxes and laws, but she was happy to hear them talk about the Handsome Prince and his doings.

When she went home, she talked to her Grandmother about the world of humans. "Why do they have all the trees and stars?" she asked, "Why can't we have trees and flowers and dancing?"

The Grandmother frowned at all her questions. "We have sea gardens and fish and dancing," she said. "We are happy here."

The Little Mermaid was too much in love to be happy. "Is there nothing I can do to change myself from a mermaid into a girl and live in the world above," she pleaded. "I want to so very much."

The Grandmother was old enough to know the value of truth, so answered the Little Mermaid's question. "I was told when I was young and had questions too, that the only way to be a girl in the world is to find a man who will love you and only you. He must worship you above all others and swear to it in a ceremony held by a man in a dress who has magic powers over birth and death. But Little Mermaid, can't you see, this is a silly tale. Men have no magic powers, no matter what they wear, and how can a man make you a girl? You are what you are and what you have always been. Stop this foolishness and come with me to the sea gardens. It's peaceful there and you don't have to be anything other than what you are. Come, child, please?"

She held out her hand to the Little Mermaid, hoping to save her from herself, knowing such a thing is never possible.

The Little Mermaid shook her head and swam away from the Grandmother. "You don't understand. I know what love is now. I hate this tail I was born with. I want legs! I want him to love me! You've never known what it is to feel this way."

Crying, she swam furiously away from the Grandmother who wanted to save her from herself and went to visit her Auntie who lived not far from her father's gardens. The Auntie had chosen to leave the Sea King's palace many years ago. She had built her own house and filled it with paintings of uncomfortable beauty. All through her sea gardens were statues she had sculpted out of pain and loss and joy and love. The Sea King didn't understand his sister and he was scared by her art that hinted at things he didn't know. He tried to keep his daughters away from her by telling them she was old and wicked, but the Little Mermaid had always loved the Auntie's truth and humour. She sought her out now in hope the Auntie could help her find a way to be a girl and love a man.

She found her Auntie painting a great canvas of entwined bodies, all green and gold. "Auntie!" she cried, "help me, please!"

The Auntie put down her brush and turned to the Little Mermaid. "I will try," she said as she hugged her close, "but I've never found trying to help people to be very helpful."

The Little Mermaid gazed up at the Auntie's large, wrinkled face. She had never lived with humans so she did not know that beauty should always be young and small and she thought the Auntie's huge round body and muscular tail were enviably beautiful.

"Auntie, I don't want to be a mermaid anymore. I want to have legs and live on land. I want the Prince to love me and live happily with me forever. What can I do?" She leaned her head against the Auntie's huge arm, strong from carving stone and fat from eating well, and drew comfort from her large strength.

The Auntie wrapped her arms around the Little Mermaid and rested her chin atop her head. She remembered what it was like to be young, to want to be something other than what she was so a man she didn't know might love her.

"The Grandmother says I can only be a girl in the world if a man will love me, but how can I get a man to love me if I cannot be a girl in the world?" the Little Mermaid asked. "Help me Auntie, I want it so much."

"I can help you get what you want," the Auntie said. "But you should know that it will hurt you terribly. You will have to take a knife and cut your beautiful tail. You can paint it to look like legs and teach you to walk on land, but the wounds will never heal. Every step you take will be as if the knife were cutting your feet again. You will bleed and hurt with every step. This is not a good thing you want, child, and it will bring you no joy."

"Oh, you're wrong Auntie," said the Little Mermaid. "All I need for joy is to look like a girl and for him to love me. I don't mind about the pain. He is worth pain. Please show me how to cut my tail and paint my legs."

"Wait!" said the Auntie, "Think! Once it is done you will not be able to undo it. If you cut your mermaid's tail to look like a girl's legs it will not heal. You will never again be a mermaid. Take some time to be sure this is the right choice."

But time takes too long for the young who have so much of it and the Little Mermaid wanted to be what she was not too much to waste time on being what she was.

The Auntie gave the Little Mermaid a knife and did not stop her from cutting her beautiful tail, because she knew that some lessons can only be learned by living them.

The Little Mermaid sliced at her tail until it split in two and used the Auntie's paint to cover her scales and scars and blood. She painted dainty little feet on the ends and laughed in delight at her new human-looking legs.

The Auntie's strong arms held her as she swam to the beach where she had left the Handsome Prince. "I want for you all you could want for yourself," she said, "but if what you want becomes a thing you do not want, come back here and call for me. I will come and help you if I can."

The Little Mermaid hugged the Auntie and thanked her. "Do not be sad Auntie, the Prince will make me so happy and I will love being a girl in the world. When I call to you it will be only to tell you of my joy." She walked slowly from the water, each step on her mutilated tail feeling like a knife cut in her new little feet.

The Little Mermaid made her way to the ornate house, leaving a trail of blood in her wake. As she approached the door it opened and the Handsome Prince stepped out. He stopped and stared in amazement at the Little Mermaid. She gazed at his handsome face and beautiful dark eyes, looking closely at every part of her. "I knew he would love me," she whispered to herself, "he looks at me as I look at him, such love, such admiration," and her smile was full of joy.

"Well look at you," said the Handsome Prince in handsome delight, "did someone send me a present? Naked girls outside my door in the morning! How wonderful."

The Little Mermaid did not know young men were taught about a girl's naked flesh and she did not understand that he thought she should feel shame, so she felt only happiness that he saw her and was pleased.

The Handsome Prince picked up the Little Mermaid and swept her off to his bedroom. What other reason would there be for girls naked outside his door in the morning?

The Little Mermaid revelled in the closeness she believed they both felt and ignored the pain that was only hers. After he was done, the Handsome Prince told her she could stay with him forever and <u>gave her permission to sleep at his door on a velvet cushion</u>.

She tried a few times to talk to the Handsome Prince, but he did not like to hear her speak. "Hush now, lovely girl," he said, "you're so much more beautiful when you listen than when you talk, has anyone ever told you that?"

No one had told the Little Mermaid this before and she was sad that she did not know how to be beautiful, but she wanted to learn, so she did her best to be silent and make herself beautiful for love.

And so, she learned to stay and dance and not speak, even though the pain was terrible and her dancing left smears of blood on the floor. Everyone in the palace knew that the blood shed by girls is too unseemly to notice, so they walked through it and over it and never spoke of it. The servants cleaned it each day and each night she would dance again.

The Handsome Prince told her many tales of how well he hunted and how much he collected in taxes and how often the people laughed when he told his jokes. He told her all about his adventures in the sea and the shipwreck from which he had swum so bravely to escape. He even told her about the Beautiful Girl he met on the beach afterwards. "She was more beautiful than you and I loved her more than I love you," he said, "but she isn't here <u>and you are like her and you have almost driven her image out of my mind. My good fortune has sent me you instead of her; and we will never be apart.</u> Maybe I might love you more one day, do you think you can make me love you more? You should try and maybe I will."

The Little Mermaid was heartbroken that he loved the Beautiful Girl more than her, but she had already given up so much for him that she couldn't give up hope as well. So she decided to stay and dance even more gracefully and listen with even more interest to his stories. Maybe one day he would love her enough.

She wanted to tell him about her garden under the sea and her sisters who loved her and her Grandmother who did not understand her and her huge beautiful Auntie who had helped her get what she wanted. But the Handsome Prince did not keep her for her voice or her story. "Dance," he cried, "Show your beauty to my friends so they can admire me."

Sometimes at night, after the Handsome Prince was done with her, the Little Mermaid would sneak out to the sand and watch her sisters playing in the breakwater at the edge of the bay. They reached out and called to her, but she didn't have her strong tail and she could not swim out to them. Her father the Sea King came to show her his anger and the Grandmother came to show her sadness, but they would not speak to her.

The Auntie came to visit her once a month. She would swim up to the beach and ask about her love and her joy. Each time the Little Mermaid steadfastly insisted that love and joy were all she had thought they would be. Each time the Auntie nodded sadly and said, "I will come back again next month."

The Auntie had come twelve times to ask about her happiness and joy and each time the Little Mermaid had said she was filled with both. Then, after the twelfth time, the Handsome Prince's father came to him to discuss his marriage. "You are the Handsome Prince of this land and my heir," he said, "You must marry a Princess who will bring riches and give you sons to rule and daughters to exchange for more riches, for this is how a Kingdom grows."

At first the Handsome Prince was reluctant because he enjoyed his life of hunting and taxing and telling jokes, and he could not see how a wife would make that better. But the King insisted and the Handsome Prince understood his job was to make more Handsome Princes with a proper wife, not a silent girl who danced, so he agreed to marry the Princess from the neighbouring kingdom.

"Don't fret," he said kindly to the Little Mermaid. "She will be just a wife and a mother. You will stay with me and dance for me because wives are not for dancing and dancing girls are not for marrying. We will all be what we are supposed to be, and you will see how happy it makes me."

The Little Mermaid wanted to tell him how much she loved him and how she had cut her tail in two so she could come and be loved by him, but he did not listen and her voice floated away on the wind.

The Handsome Prince and all his courtiers and servants boarded a new boat and sailed to the neighbouring kingdom to collect the Princess who would be his bride. The Little Mermaid came too because the Handsome Prince liked to watch her dance. She cried and danced and bled and all the Handsome Prince's friends cheered and admired him for her beauty.

The night before they landed at the neighbouring kingdom the Little Mermaid had finished dancing and submitting. "I wish I did not have to marry a Princess," said the Handsome Prince, "if I cannot marry the Beautiful Girl who you resemble, I would rather marry you, my silent foundling." And then <u>he kissed her rosy mouth, played with her long waving hair, and laid his head on her heart, while she dreamed of human happiness</u> and listened to him as he explained to her about the sea she had known her whole life.

When they arrived at the neighbouring kingdom the Princess was brought out to greet the Handsome Prince and he was shocked to discover that she was none other than the Beautiful Girl who had helped him off the beach after he swam so bravely from the shipwreck.

The Handsome Prince was overjoyed to see her. "I have waited all this time for you," he cried. "I have had no one to listen to my stories or share my bed. Now we can be together forever. How wonderful that you are to marry me, and everyone can admire me for your beauty."

The Beautiful Girl who was also a Princess understood her role in any story was to be beautiful and fertile and unselfish, so she smiled at the Handsome Prince and allowed him to believe whatever he wished.

The Handsome Prince and the Beautiful Princess married on the deck of the ship. The Little Mermaid smiled prettily and carried the bridal train for the Beautiful Princess. She watched as all the courtiers danced and sang and laughed. She thought of the first time she had seen the Handsome Prince and the dancing and laughing, so long ago, on the night of the storm. She danced for them all, more graceful and elegant than ever. Everyone cheered her as her tender feet bled onto the ship's deck and she thought of her beautiful voice and how she used to sing and talk and swim through the waves with her sisters. She looked at the Handsome Prince, who was telling his stories to the Beautiful Princess now. Her silence and her pain and her losses were too much.

She went to the edge of the ship and looked out over the sea. "He will never give me happiness or joy. My tail is gone and these silly legs will not carry me through the waves anymore. But I would rather go back and die than stay here and live in silence and pain." She climbed over the edge of the ship, her little feet aching and bleeding, and threw herself into the waves.

As she sank beneath the surface she cried again, not for the Handsome Prince this time but for herself, for everything she had given up and for the happiness she had thought she could only have with him.

Just as she thought she was finally about to die, huge strong arms wrapped around her and a loving voice said "My darling one, you have returned. What have you to tell me of happiness and joy?"

It was the Auntie, holding her close and swimming with her back to her garden and her sisters. She clung to the Auntie's big beautiful body and spilled out all her secrets and shame. Her voice grew stronger and louder as she talked about her dancing and her bleeding and her silence. She told the Auntie about the Handsome Prince and his stories that she finally understood were lies and his jokes that were only cruelty. She talked and the Auntie listened and loved and shared her pain. As they swam together and the Little Mermaid shed her shame, the painted legs slowly washed off in the sea. The Auntie smoothed over the cuts with healing hands and her tail began to mend.

"You will never again be what you were before you cut your tail into legs and turned your voice into silence," the Auntie told her. "But you will grow strong again. You will be who you are and you will find happiness and joy in that. You can stay here in your sea garden with your sisters if you want. Or you can leave again and find other places to be yourself. Your tail will always carry the scars of the cuts you made but they will not mar your beauty, they will always tell the story of what you can survive. Be proud of them and of yourself."

"Will I really find happiness and joy, Auntie? Will I be loved? Will someone want me for my scarred tail and my voice and what I know about the sea?"

"I will. You will. Your sisters will. And many others too. One person cannot share all your pain or all your joy. But you will have many people to love you and be loved by you. It's not everything, but it is a great deal."

The Little Mermaid, having lived in the world as a girl which brings wisdom that cannot be found any other way, laughed a little and cried a little and flipped her tail.

"The Handsome Prince," she said, "what a fool he was. Such a waste of my time and silence and pain."

The Auntie laughed a little and cried a little too. "Yes my darling, he truly was."

This story ends here but the Little Mermaid had a long life, full of many joys and sorrows.

Beauty and the Beast: Part 1 A Tale As Old As Time

This is not another fun re-write of an old fairy tale. As much as I enjoyed giving Cinderella, Sleeping Beauty and the Little Mermaid a new story, I didn't change Beauty's fate. The original is a dark story about coercive control - and so is my version.

All variations of Beauty and the Beast share some similarities with the story written down by Gabrielle-Suzanne Barbot de Villeneuve in 1740. In her version, a man who was once rich loses his wealth and goes on a journey to recover some of what he lost. His older daughters send him on his way with requests for jewels and sumptuous dresses. The youngest daughter is too sweet and unselfish to ask for material goods; she wants a simple flower. The rich man's quest is unsuccessful, but on his way home he finds an empty manor, filled with warm beds and good food. He stays the night and takes a flower from the garden on his way out to give to his deserving youngest daughter. The Beast appears and threatens to kill him, not for taking the food and shelter but for taking the flower he could not possibly have known was forbidden to him. The man begs for his life and the Beast asks for one of his daughters as restitution. The man offers his youngest and most beautiful daughter, and she is brought to the Beast's castle. Her older sisters, jealous of the wealth the Beast gives her, persecute her in various ways, proving they are unworthy of the love of a Handsome Prince. During the day, The Beast frightens her and asks her to marry him. She refuses and each night she dreams about a Handsome Prince. She asks the Beast if she can visit her family and he is heartbroken that she wants to see anyone other than him, but he gives her permission to go. While she is at home being happy, she dreams again of the Handsome Prince, who is crying and says he will die because she left him. She returns to the Beast and agrees to marry him. Her unselfishly steadfast love breaks the enchantment, and the beast is revealed to be a Handsome Prince.

This story has been teaching little girls throughout history and all over the world that love can transform frightening men into the man of your dreams. That you will get your Happy Ever After if you are good enough and love him enough. That if he continues to be beastly, it is only because you do not deserve anything else. Try harder!

As much as I wanted to free Beauty from this trap, I think it's more useful to tell the story of a young woman trapped in a relationship with a controlling man because we all need to remember that every man is as good or bad as he chooses to be.

Once upon a time there lived a Merchant who had three daughters. He was very rich. He was proud that he had never needed help to become so, all he started with was his father's wealth, his grandfather's land, and his brother's friends. "I earned my success," he said, "and I do not deserve to fail."

One day, after many years of success without failure, he foolishly sent all his ships out into a storm, and none came back. In a very short time all father's wealth and his grandfather's land were sold to pay his debts and his brother's friends refused to remember a man who reminded them that they too could fail.

The Merchant wailed for his lost riches and berated his daughters for the profligacy he had taught them. But a few weeks later, a messenger came with news that one single ship might have survived the storm. The Merchant went to say farewell to his daughters. "My last ship may come in," he told them. "What shall I bring you if it does?"

"Jewels," said the oldest. "Silks," said the next. The youngest and most beautiful daughter asked for nothing but a rose, because she was not like other girls.

The Merchant walked and walked and walked to the port, but it was all for nothing. His last ship had not come in. He had nothing left of his father's wealth or his grandfather's land. His brother's friends gave him only pity and, in exchange, took comfort that they had been too clever to lose all their ships in the storm.

Alone, bereft, he walked and walked and walked towards home and the daughters who needed jewels and silks to be beautiful and the beautiful daughter who needed only a rose because she was not like other girls.

"What do I do?" he asked himself. "The night is getting colder and I am getting older and there is no money or work. Who am I if I am not man enough to do a man's work and have a man's wealth?"

Shining through the darkness, he saw lights from a castle. "Shelter!" he said. "Perhaps there is someone in the castle who will take comfort from my poverty and give me food in exchange."

The castle was full of light and luxury and echoes, but there was no one there. The Merchant found a table laden with food and ate his fill. He found a soft bed with clean sheets and took his rest upon it. In the morning, as he ate his fill again, he wondered why so much was given to an empty castle full of empty rooms.

"This castle should not be empty," he said. "I, who was born to wealth and lands, who earned my success and did not deserve my failure, I have a right to take this for myself. It would not be stealing to take this because I know how to be a man of wealth and taste. I will bring my daughters here and put them in these rooms where they will look beautiful, and I will have all that I deserve once more."

Happy with his choice to be wealthy again, The Merchant wandered out to the garden. He found a rose bush and remembered that his youngest, most beautiful daughter had asked only for a flower. So he picked a perfect rose, perfect for a girl who, unlike other girls, did not ask for perfection.

As he picked it, a man appeared before him. A towering, angry man, beast-like in his rage. "How dare you?" the beast-like man thundered. "My food you took because you did not think I was here, and I said nothing! My bed you took because you did not think I was here, and I said nothing. Now you take my perfect rose because you did not think I was here, and you expect me to say nothing? Nothing? I will kill you for this!"

The Beast advanced on The Merchant, his hands clawed in rage. "Beg me for your life!" he said.

The Merchant begged and The Beast laughed. "Begging will not give you your life. Plead on your knees for your life."

The Merchant fell to his knees and pleaded for his life. The Beast laughed and wrapped his hands around the Merchant's neck. "Pleading will not give you your life. Tell me why you wanted my rose. Such a weak and womanly thing for a man to want."

"I am a man. I did not want your rose. It's for my daughter. She is young and beautiful, she is not like other girls and all she asked for was one perfect rose," The Merchant wept.

The Beast paused. "A beautiful girl who is not like other girls? I am a man and like all men, I want such a girl. Give her to me and I will give you your life."

The Merchant knew a girl's life, even a girl who is not like other girls, is not a valuable thing. Not like the life of a man who earned his success and did not deserve his failure. So he agreed to give his daughter to The Beast.

The Beast smiled a hideous smile and released him. They returned to the castle where The Beast piled jewels and silks in the back of gleaming horses. "Give these to your oldest daughters," he said. "Give the rose to your youngest daughter. Make sure she knows that if she does not come to me, I will come to you. I will take the jewels and silks and horses, then I will take your life. I will do it while she watches. Do not forget. She must know the price you will all pay if you do not give her to me."

The Merchant promised to tell his youngest, most beautiful daughter all these things and hurried home.

His oldest daughters, who were just like other girls, were delighted to see the horses laden with jewels and silks. The youngest daughter took her perfect rose and hugged her father. "I am so glad you are home safely," she said.

"Do not be glad," The Merchant told her. "I am here with a terrible choice for you. I met a man, a beast of a man, who gave me the jewels, the silks, the horses, the rose, and my life. In return he asked only for you. If you do not go to him, he will come here. He will take everything we have left and kill me horribly while you watch. He wants you to know he can and will do this. I am a good man, not a beast, so even though I have promised to give you to him, I will give you a choice. Do you want your sisters who, like other girls, care only for jewels and silks, to lose everything? Do you want your father who does not deserve to fail, to be killed horribly as you watch? Or will you freely choose to give yourself to The Beast?"

His youngest daughter, who was too young and beautiful and unselfish to be like other girls, made her choice that was no choice and agreed to live with The Beast.

When she arrived at the castle, The Beast was delighted to see her. "You are indeed the most beautiful girl!" he crowed. "So young! Such skin! Such eyes! I will call you Beauty because that is the only thing about you that matters. I will buy you a new dress because that one you wear is not good enough. You will grow your hair long because your hair is too short and that is the only flaw I can see in you. I will tell you everything about me, all the things I have never told anyone because I was waiting for you to know the real me and be the only person who can love me enough that I no longer need to be such a beast. Come. Let me show you how much I love you."

The Beast swept Beauty up in his arms and carried her up the stairs to show her how much he loved her.

Beauty and the Beast lived together in the castle for months. The Beast taught her to wear the clothes he liked so she would be the beauty he knew she could be. He knew she did not know how to manage money for herself, so kept money away from her. Beauty learned that her laugh was too loud and her tears caused him pain, so she did not laugh or cry. The Beast taught her that her ideas were too silly and her dreams were too much, and he gave her all of his to hold instead of her own. He taught her to value how much she was not like other girls, those vain, selfish, silly other girls who wanted for themselves instead of others, and she knew she was special because she wanted only for him.

As he made her cut away all the pieces of herself and replace them with pieces of him, Beauty kept only one desire of her own. She wanted to see her family again.

"But why?" asked The Beast. "Your father gave you to me. Do you think he would do that if he wanted you? Your sisters are like all the other girls. They are cruel and shallow and selfish. They don't understand love like you do. They won't understand us. You know how much I need you. Why do you want to leave me alone? Do you not care how much you hurt me?"

Beauty did care about The Beast. She did not want to hurt him and so she stayed with him even when he hurt her. She hid her pain from him because he told her it would hurt him to see it. She hid her pain from everyone else because he told her that everything of her, even her pain, belonged to him.

Her sisters, though, did not know how much it hurt the Beast when Beauty cared about other people. They were too silly and selfish to care only about the Beast and they wanted to see Beauty. They wrote letters she could not answer lest it hurt the Beast. They knocked at the door she could not open lest it hurt the Beast. Worst of all, they visited the local village and asked questions about the Beast and how he treated Beauty.

Every day the Beast told Beauty that he could not stand to be away from her for even a minute. She could not sleep unless he was there. She could not read, she could not sing, she could not even look at the art on the wall because it hurt the Beast to see her ignore him so. Once a week, however, the Beast had to go to the village to do business with traders who met at the tavern. Sometimes this meant he had to leave Beauty alone for days at a time and he taught her to feel sad for him that he had to be away from her so long.

The village traders were clever and important men. In their pride and delight that such a great lord would descend from his castle to make merry with the Butcher, the Baker, and the Candlestick Maker, they saw only the man and not the Beast.

One day the Beast returned from the village full of rage. "Why are your sisters saying terrible things about me? Why are women in the village listening to them? Why are they asking questions about you? What did you do? You must have told them something. Why do you tell lies about me?" The Beast's rage was a terrible thing.

Beauty wept and bled and wept some more.

"How could I tell them anything about you? I do not speak to them. I love you. I only talk to you because I know it hurts you when I need anyone else."

The Beast raged on. "Liar! Faithless whore!" he screamed. Overwhelmed by betrayal, he lost himself in his fury. Beauty wept and bled and grieved for him.

The next day the Beast held her tenderly in his arms. "I love you", he crooned, "You know how I love you. You're The One I waited for. The only one who could know me and love me. I want you to see your sisters. Even if being without you hurts me until I want to die, I want you to go to them. Don't try to explain us to them. They see the Beast. You're the only one who knows I could be the Handsome Prince of your dreams. Keep that for us alone. Don't profane it by trying to show it to those others who can never understand our perfect love."

Beauty understood. She wasn't like the other girls who had hurt the Beast and made him into a man who hurt her. She was special. She would keep his love for herself alone.

The Beast sent Beauty to see her sisters and because he loved her, he told her not to stay too long or say too much or trust them at all.

At first, Beauty obeyed him as she always did. As the days went by, she watched her sisters setting jewels into intricately crafted chains and weaving silks into elaborate tapestries and planning beautiful new designs and exchanged them for money and food. She listened as they like so many other girls, talked about their plans and dreams and growth. She tried to share her dreams too, but she had given all of hers to the Beast and her sisters were not interested in her dreams for him.

"We love you, little sister," they said. "We care about you, and you are more than just him. Tell us about you."

But the Beast had taught her too well and Beauty did not know how to belong to herself, she only knew how to be his.

Every day The Beast sent letters to Beauty begging her to come home. "I miss you. I love you. I cannot live without you. What are you saying to your sisters? Why are they keeping us apart when they know how it hurts me? I will die if you do not come home soon."

Beauty told her oldest sister that the Beast would die without her, but the oldest sister laughed and said, "Oh, silly! We haven't seen you for months. Surely if he wants you to be happy he will want you to spend time with the family who loves you."

Another day. More letters. "I will die without you. I want to die if you are not here. Come back to me. Please."

Beauty told her next oldest sister that the Beast would die without her, but her next oldest sister laughed, and said, "Oh, silly! No one dies from being left alone for a few days. Isn't he happy for you that you get to see your family after so long being away from us?"

Beauty was sad that her sisters didn't understand true love as she had learned it from The Beast. But she stayed with her sisters and started to remember what it was like to be hers instead of his.

Another day another letter. "I thought you loved me. I thought your love was enough to turn me into your Handsome Prince. Don't you love me enough for me to be a good man? I love you much more than that so I will give you another choice: Stay there and be like all the other girls and I will kill myself horribly while you are not here to watch. Or come back to me and I will live and maybe one day I will become your Handsome Prince. The choice is yours."

Beauty left her home that day and returned to the Beast. He had not killed himself horribly while she was not there to watch, but he assured her that he would have. "You must never leave me again," he said as he held her close. "I love you too much to let you leave. Marry me, Beauty, and we will live happily ever after."

Beauty made another choice that was no choice and they were married the next day. They both lived... for a while.

Beauty and the Beast: Part 2 Happily Ever After

Fairy tales always end when the princess marries her Handsome Prince because a wedding is a fairy tale. Marriage is not. At its best, marriage is a partnership between equals. A shared life of trust, companionship, and compromise in the service of mutual happiness. At its worst, marriage is a malevolent ouroboros of fear, shame, and violence. Most of us embark on marriage believing we will have the fairy tale, the best of the best. Too many of us discover too late that we've married the Beast and we cannot love him into being a better man. How easily can we walk away from the dream of the happy ever after and our belief that we earned our fairy tale princess ending? And what does the world say to us if we do? Or even if we don't?

This book is about fairy tales, not the separate but related genre of nursery rhymes. But as I was writing it, this old children's rhyme kept cycling through my mind:

> Rub a dub dub,
> Three fools in a tub,
> And who do you think they be?
> The Butcher, the Baker,
> The Candlestick Maker.
> Turn them out, knaves all three!
> *Old English Nursery Rhyme, Origins unknown*

Like most nursery rhymes, Rub a dub dub originated in the middle ages. The tub refers to an old fairground attraction where scantily clad or even naked women would sit in a bathtub for men to ogle in a 14th century version of a modern strip club. The Butcher, the Baker, and the Candlestick Maker symbolised the supposedly respectable tradesmen who would try to sneak into the tub with the women.

In the 18th and 19th century, the phrase "the Butcher, the Baker, the Candlestick Maker" was often used to denote the rapidly expanding class of respectable tradesmen. They were the Everyman, who, individually did not have much power but as a group they played a significant role in determining the social rules of the British Empire. In modern terms they might be the Tradie, the Accountant, and the Sales Manager. They could be of any age or gender; their primary characteristic is their ordinariness and the appearance of respectability. They infest comment sections of all online spaces, proving their own worthiness by their condemnation of "bad" women and sincerely believe that this worthiness transforms threats of violence and rape into righteous invective against evil.

The Wedding Day

The Butcher: "A wedding! Haha! He was finally caught! Who'd have thought such a man could be chained? He's a wild man, a strong man, a man's man, no doubt. A pretty girl like that might settle him down. Keep him calm, make him happy, give him peace. A wife and some young 'uns, that's just what he needs. She'll have to work hard though, that man (what a man) he's a hard dog to keep on the porch."

The Baker: "Work hard! She won't bother. She doesn't fool me. She can smile and giggle like a cute little girl, but I know, I can tell, I can see. It's all just an act. She's a gold-digger, a harpy, a conniving young slut. She'll take all his coins and castles and jewels, she'll leave him with nothing, just you wait, just you wait, just you see."

The Candlestick Maker: "He told me in secret, just once, just us two. He doubts her sometimes, you know? So pretty, so kind, so beautifully sweet. What is she hiding? What doesn't she tell him? What does he need to know?"

All: "Poor man, poor man, how did he get caught? Oh, what a terrible fate awaits him."

Five years later

The Butcher: "That girl they called Beauty, who married the Prince. She's really let herself go. She used to laugh all the time, but she doesn't no more. Doesn't talk, doesn't smile, doesn't skip down the road. Why is she so sad and sour?"

The Baker: "Thinks too much of herself, that stuck-up fat bitch. Too high and mighty, she is. I've tried, just a little, because I don't care what she thinks, to have a joke and a laugh. But no, she won't smile at a good man like me. Just hides in that castle, being sulky and glum. She's lucky he stays. No wonder he strays. He could do better for himself, so he could, so he could, so he should."

The Candlestick Maker: "He told me one time, when we were alone, quite alone. She's gone a little bit mad. Makes up lies, always cries. Drinks alone and too much. He doesn't know what to do."

All: "Poor man, poor man, how did he get caught? Oh, what a terrible fate awaits him."

Ten years later

The Butcher: "She's not a good wife to that wonderful man. She told lies to my wife and my girls. Said he hurt her and beat her, what nonsense she spills. I know what happened. I know the truth! Some trinkets she wanted, some bauble or gewgaw he'd never deny. But it wasn't big enough, he wasn't quick enough. And now she believes she's abused."

The Baker: "That harpy, that fishwife, that hellcat on wheels. What does she want from him now? That's what they do, those jaded old shrews. They lie to good women and wives who stay true. Try to whip up a storm against good men who've done nothing! He could kick her to the kerb and take his pick of young girls, so he could, so he could, so he should."

The Candlestick Maker: "He confided in me, only once, just one time. She's got nothing left of womanly warmth, of kindness or softness or ardour. Her bed is as cold as her heart and her head. He lies there and suffers alone."

All: "Poor man, poor man, how did he get caught? Oh, what a terrible fate awaits him."

Fifteen years later

The Butcher: "My wife told me last night, a terrible tale. Says that Beauty took off with his coins and his son. He had to chase her for miles, poor man, and drag her straight home. She fought like a wildcat, scratched his face and his hands. The wife saw it today and of course thought the worst. Some women love drama and gossip and shock. That's all there was to it, I'll stake my life. Just lies and a crazy old shrew."

The Baker: "What did I tell you? What did I say? She was only ever after his gold. She got what she wanted, his gold and his child. She'll leave him with nothing and laugh while she does it, that's what women do. He needs to teach her a lesson, one she'll never forget, so he could, so he could, so he should."

The Candlestick Maker: "He told me once, just a secret, just for me, just for him, that she lies every time she speaks. Day and night she tells lies and it just breaks his heart. So sad that he can't let her go."

All: "Poor man, poor man, how did he get caught? Oh, what a terrible fate awaits him."

Twenty years later

The Butcher: "Did you hear? Do you know? I'm all of a dither! She is dead! She is dead! And it was him that killed her! Old Tom saw him do it! With his very own eyes! Or

I'd never have swallowed such terrible lies. He watched unbelieving, couldn't know what he was seeing. The king choked his wife till she died! Why didn't she leave him? Why did she stay? She should have told someone. What a terrible waste."

The Baker: "What did she do to make him so mad? How did she turn a good man so bad? Now watch as he pays for the rest of his life. This is what women can do. They ruin your life if you let them get close. He could tell the truth about what she was really like, so he could, so he could, so he should."

The Candlestick Maker: "He told me one time, just me no one else, that he loved her so much he could die. He won't want to live, no he won't, not without her. He'll be lost, he's alone, he's got no one now."

All: "Poor man, poor man, how did he get caught? Oh, what a terrible fate awaits him."

The End

Afterword

Wow. Bleak, huh?

Fairy tale princesses do not live a good life. I did think about rewriting all of them so they could have that good life but peeling back the veneer to see the ugliness underneath doesn't work if you erase the ugliness before you begin. So, some of my princesses had to follow the path laid down for them by the men who wrote their stories. It helps us see it more clearly when women, girls, non-binary people tell new stories. Even Disney has done it – yes, hello *Encanto* – but so many others have done it too. *The Good Wife, Deadloch*, Elizabeth Acevedo, Tarana Burke, Yassmin Abdel-Magied, Hannah Gadsby, Amanda Gorman, the list goes on and on.

We need to tell great stories for women and girls. And celebrate the best of them. We need to share them and talk about them and *pay for them* (when we can). We need to keep proving to the people who make money from stories that great stories about women will make money. Beyoncé, the Matildas, Barbie, and Taylor Swift have made 2023 a bumper year but the (mostly) men who make investment decisions about the stories we're given are sometimes a bit slow to understand that women are real people. Remind them. The stories don't have to be happy or easy. They just have to be good. The two things you need to make good stories are time and money. Let's make it easier for women, girls, and non-binary people to get the time, money and support they need to tell us those great stories. No one needs any more lazy "Beautiful Princess and her Handsome Prince" rubbish. We can do so much better than that.